"That's sweet, Chase." She was sitting in the chair next to him and leaned over and kissed his cheek. She hadn't meant to. It was unconscious really, but her lips sought out his face. They lingered on his smooth skin, just a moment too long. He smelled good. Clean. Expensive. With a little bit of the heavenly scent of the bakery lingering on him.

She lifted her lips away, tried to back away before she got caught up, before she wasn't able to make herself back away. But it was already too late. Because Chase slid his hand along her cheek and brought her face closer to his.

He kissed her. Not hot and fiery like she might have wanted, but slow and deep like she needed. That kiss gave her another glimpse inside of him. It told her how he might be as her lover, in her bed. He would take his time just like he was taking his time now, kissing her thoroughly, not leaving any part of her mouth untasted.

Dear Reader,

In *Love and a Latte*, you'll meet Chase and Amber, a couple who proves that opposites really do attract. The conservative accountant and the bohemian jewelry-designing beauty realize that they have much more in common than the world thinks. Even though Chase's family isn't so sure about the match, he'll do anything to prove that Amber is the right woman for him.

I hope you enjoy reading about them as much as I enjoyed writing about them.

Happy reading,

Jamie

Love And a Latte

JAMIE POPE

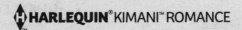

HARLEQUIN® KIMANI™ ROMANCE

Special thanks and acknowledgment are given to Jamie Pope for her contribution to The Draysons: Sprinkled with Love

Recycling programs
for this product may
not exist in your area.

ISBN-13: 978-0-373-86458-4

Love and a Latte

Printed in U.S.A.

Jamie Pope first fell in love with romance when her mother placed a novel in her hands at the age of thirteen. She became addicted to love stories and has been writing them ever since. When she's not writing her next book, you can find her shopping for shoes or binge-watching shows on Netflix.

Books by Jamie Pope

Harlequin Kimani Romance

Surrender at Sunset
Love and a Latte

Visit the Author Profile page
at Harlequin.com for more titles.

To my father, James.
Just because he likes having books dedicated to him.

Acknowledgments

Pamela and Yahrah, thanks for putting up with
the dozens upon dozens of emails.

Chapter 1

Numbers were always something Chase Drayson excelled at. They were the only things in the world that always made sense to him. They were concrete. Always easy for him to figure out, to play with. He was unlike his sister and brother, who were good at those intangible things. Immeasurable things. Creative things like dealing with people and coming up with outside-of-the-box ideas that Chase just couldn't wrap his head around. That's why he'd spent his entire career in corporate finance. Growing the profits of the businesses he worked for as well as creating wealth for himself.

People who didn't know him well might call him money hungry. But he didn't like the phrase because it implied that he was greedy. He wasn't. He'd just always liked to work. Earn for himself instead of being handed things. The summer he turned eight, he ran his neighborhood's only lemonade stand, creating a market analysis summary complete with potential growth in his target markets. At fourteen he had organized a team of teenage lawn mowers who'd made more profit that quarter than one local landscaping company. And by seventeen he was doing pretty swift business employing his friends and classmates to walk dogs and feed the cats of his vacationing neighbors.

He definitely wasn't money hungry. He didn't buy diamond-encrusted watches or spend foolishly on flashy things with little value that he didn't need. He was hungry for organization and structure. Hungry to see something that he managed grow into the something big and successful. He liked to know that his money was working for him. Know that each hour he invested was going to pay off tenfold.

He wasn't sure how other people could go through life not doing that. People who were content just to sit back and let things happen for them. People who could just go where the wind blew them. The thought of that made Chase shudder. That's why he was sitting in the café section of his family's new bakery, Lillian's of Seattle, far past closing time, going over the finances. Again. Tweaking the business plan. Studying the market analysis summary he had created.

They were doing well by most people's standards. They'd had a successful opening month and were on track to maintain steady business. His parents thought he and his siblings were crazy for deciding to take on the running of a bakery when they had no experience.

They were old-school, wanting their children to only have careers with steady incomes that they could always count on, but Chase, Jackson and Mariah Drayson sometimes had to ignore the well-intentioned advice of their parents.

They had to take this calculated risk because Chase knew it could really pay off. And besides, running a bakery seemed to be in their blood. Their extended family had been doing so in Chicago for two generations and were starting to branch out around the country.

His baby sister had left her job in advertising to bake for them after her divorce was final. She was surprisingly excellent at it. And a creative force, too, inventing the Draynut, a combination of a croissant and doughnut that people were going wild for. Mariah was bringing customers in by the droves and her creation was the boost their small business needed. But Chase knew all about fads and trends, and while things were going well now, they could crash and burn in no time. He knew that even businesses with successful openings had a high risk of failing in the first year.

In every job that Chase worked, he always did his best to succeed, but making Lillian's a success was more important to him than any other job he had ever had. Because Lillian's was all about family and tradition. The Seattle shop was the third bakery. The original, started by the Chicago branch of his family and run now by his cousins, was an institution in the Windy City. He wanted the Seattle shop to have the same legacy as the original.

He secretly wanted it to be better than the original.

It was a challenge. He hadn't had a real challenge in a long time. That's why when Mariah sprung this idea on him, even though he was apprehensive, he agreed. As the eldest he felt it was his job to make sure this place flourished.

Chase had done his research. He knew an upscale, well-positioned bakery could do well in Seattle. It could outearn the original bakery if managed properly and he knew of no better man for the job than him. So he had taken a leave of absence from work and thrown everything he had into making Lillian's a success. The only thing that was sticking in his side was the competition.

Sweetness Bakery. It had dominated the market in Seattle, and for the life of him, Chase couldn't figure out why. He had gotten pastries there himself once or twice. But from what he remembered there was nothing exceptional about them. Nothing that made him want to go back. Not the decor. Not the coffee. Not the customer service.

Lillian's was superior to them in every way. The homey, elegant interior. The superior coffee from their new partner, Myers Coffee Roasters, and the stomach-growling sweet smells from the pastries put them leaps and bounds above the competition. Even though the bakery was closed now, the scent of fine coffee and great baked goods stayed with him.

And it was then he realized that a large steaming coffee concoction and a plate of chocolate-drizzled butter popcorn cookies had been slid in front of him.

"It looks like you could use this," he heard a soft, feminine voice say. He looked up to see a woman standing in front of him. She was the barista. He had noticed her before because she was cute. Petite but curvy with beautiful smooth brown skin and a head full of bouncy curls. And she always wore something bright. Yellow. Orange. Pink. She didn't seem like the type of girl who hid in corners. And she was smiling at him now. That's what he remembered the most about her, the way she smiled at their customers. Warm and welcoming. It was a smile that made a person feel at home. She was the kind of employee that they needed at Lillian's. But for the life of him he couldn't remember her name.

"Thank you…"

Annie?

Amy?

Ashley.

"You don't remember my name, do you, Mr. Chase Drayson? Oldest of the Drayson siblings. Wharton School of Business grad and Mr. Money-Guy. I think I'm hurt." She flashed him a smile he could only describe as flirty while she took the seat across from him. "I'm Amber. Amber Bernard. We've met before. I work here. In the bakery. As the barista. Remember?"

She had great eyes, too. Wide. Almond shaped. Almost innocent-looking. They kind of sparkled when she smiled. "That much I do remember. I'm sorry." He felt a beat of attraction that wasn't expected. He'd never thought he had a type, but she wasn't the usual sort of woman he was drawn to with her flirty smile and funky style. He couldn't help but take note of the flowy top and snug, body-hugging jeans she wore. "I was caught up in work. Everything else seems to fade away when I am."

"I could tell. I was doing the cancan right in front of you for fifteen minutes."

She smiled at him again and this time he smiled back. "Really? I'm sorry I missed that. It must have been quite a show."

"It was." She held her head haughtily, which caused him to laugh. "I may have short legs, but these girls can kick."

Amber watched Chase as he picked up his steaming mug and took a long sip.

Good Lord, he's a beautiful man.

And he was, when his head wasn't buried in his laptop. She wasn't surprised that he didn't remember her. Every time she saw him, he was busy working or talking about work or walking around deep in thought. And she knew those thoughts must be about work, too. He was the most serious of the Drayson siblings. Mariah, who had become her friend, was sweet, creative and lovely. Jackson was personable and a flirt, but Chase... She didn't know much about Chase except he worked hard, and his siblings not only loved him, but looked up to him. He was a brilliant, successful guy. It was written all over him.

"So how are things?" she asked him when he put his cup down.

"With the business? Or personally?" He nodded toward the mug. "That is excellent, by the way. What is it?"

"I call it caramel brûlé coffee. Made with milk, caramel sauce, brown sugar and whipped cream."

"I like it."

"I thought you would. A lot of men drink their coffee black because they think it's manly, but I can tell you are a man who likes some things sweet."

He gave her another smile showing off his perfectly white, perfectly straight teeth. He was just a beautiful man all around, and now that Amber was sitting right across from him she could see how handsome he was up close.

Handsome but buttoned up. Literally. It was late and yet he sat there looking almost as pristine as he did when he'd walked in that morning. She had the urge to rumple him up. Get him a little messy. Pop a few buttons on his shirt. Maybe see a bit of that big strong chest he was hiding under there.

There was no doubt she found him attractive. Not that she was interested or anything. She didn't mix business with pleasure, and he was technically her boss. But she found him beautiful like an artist might find a sculpture beautiful. All fine lines and strong curves.

"Have a cookie." She slid the plate closer to him. She should have just left after she cleaned up, like she had every other time she'd closed the bakery. She should have just gone home, but the only thing she really had to look forward to there was a textbook with her name on it. It was all a part of getting her MBA.

"I thought Mariah was crazy when she told me she wanted to put these on the menu." He took a bite. "But they're good."

"Your sister is amazingly creative. It's not work for her to create these recipes. She really thinks it's fun."

"Fun." He nodded. "That sounds like my sister."

"We've become good friends. I used to work for Everett at another location of Myers. I'm glad they ended up together." Mariah had fallen in love with Amber's widowed former boss and his young son and she was truly happy for them. Both of them had faced a lot of tragedy in their pasts, but they were on their way to becoming a wonderful little family. "She mentioned planning a vacation for them all after the Bite of Seattle festival in a couple of months."

"She deserves it." He nodded.

"What about you? You work hard." She took a cookie off the plate and sunk her teeth into it. Butter and chocolate. Sweet-and-salty perfection. "Mmm." She shut her eyes for a moment and just savored the decadent treat. She had worked around pastry for a long time, but the pastries at Lillian's were enough to make anyone go off their diet.

"If that's what you look like when you eat a cookie, then I wonder what you look like when…you do other enjoyable things."

Her eyes popped open when she heard Chase's voice. He was looking at her. Staring, really, and she felt self-conscious. Which was odd for her. Men didn't normally make her feel that way, but Chase Drayson did. "Do you have any fun summer plans?"

"No." He shook his head. "I plan on working."

"Working? That's incredibly disappointing."

"Not to me. I like to work."

She believed him. He looked like one of those men who lived for the opportunity to be chained to a desk.

He was so different from her—who merely thought of a life sitting behind a desk and broke out in hives. "You can't spend your whole life working. You might explode one day, or worse, look back on life when you're an old man and regret that you didn't live your life to the fullest."

"You must think I'm a stuffy old son of a bitch."

"I don't," she said truthfully. Sitting across from him in the dimly lit store, she could see how attractive he was, how tall he held himself, how his clothes fit his hard body The words *stuffy* and *old* hadn't come to mind. "But I think if you spend your life only working and never playing that you'll turn into one."

"I went on safari last year. It was one of the greatest experiences of my life. I live," he said, his voice kind of low and sexy. "I work hard so I can live the life I want to. If I have any regrets, not enjoying my life wouldn't be one of them."

"A safari?" That surprised her. "I've always wanted to do that." He had a little bit of adventure inside him. Maybe Mr. Workaholic played as hard as he worked, and she found that extremely interesting. "Tell me what it was like."

His eyes got this almost far-off dreamy look and she knew he was picturing the journey in his mind. "I don't know if there are strong enough words to describe it."

"Try." She wanted to be inside his head in that moment. She wanted to be with him as he saw again what he'd experienced.

"It was a ten-day trip," he started. "And each day was better than the one before. I went on the Skyline in a

tiny gondola to the top of the mountain. You feel like
you are literally on top of the world and nothing and no
one can stop you from doing anything you have ever
wanted to do. The sea is below you, and butterflies and
birds are flying around you and there are lizards sun-
ning themselves on the rocks. And you remember that
nature is the most beautiful thing ever created and no
man or machine could ever make anything as beautiful."

"Sounds incredible." She could almost see it. The
way he spoke about his trip, the sound of his soft, deep
voice combined with the descriptions kind of mesmerized her, kind of floated around and soothed her. He
should narrate a movie. He should tell more stories. He
had a beautiful voice even if it was a quiet one and she
wanted to hear him speak more.

"That was just the first day. We went to the Cape of
Good Hope and to Boulders Beach to see the penguins.
And then there was a tour of the primate sanctuary."

"Stop. Just stop before I die of jealousy." She clutched
her heart dramatically. "A primate sanctuary. Please tell
me you have pictures."

He shook his head, laughing. "Hundreds of them. I
didn't get to the actual safari part yet."

"Save it. We'll need something to talk about the next
time I close up and you work late." As soon as the words
left her mouth, she knew she was inviting herself to get
to know him better, inviting herself to see him again.
It was a mistake. She'd come over here because he was
so hard at work and he was her good friend's brother,
who she knew next to nothing about, and she wanted
him to pull his eyes off his screen and put them on her.

She hadn't counted on being mesmerized by his deep chocolaty voice or slightly turned-on by the way his lips formed words, by the way his eyes lit when he talked about something he was passionate about. "I've got to get home anyway and hit the books."

"The books?" He seemed genuinely curious. "What are you studying?"

"I'm in grad school. Going for my MBA. I'm an artist, or a jewelry designer, to be exact. I'm focusing on marketing and branding." She lifted the intricately wire-wrapped pendant that was nestled between her breasts. "I specialize in wire work."

He grabbed her wrist, lifting it closer to his face and she felt tingles rush up her arm and travel all over her body at his touch. It was unexpected and a little exciting. But it wasn't the kind of excitement she needed in her life right now.

"You made these, too?" He studied the gold wire bracelets on her wrists. "This one says your name. I don't think I'm likely to forget it anymore." He ran his thumb over it. The sensation of his warm thumb combined with the smooth metal against her skin made her heart beat just a little faster. "Very impressive, Miss Amber. You're the real deal, aren't you? I don't have a creative bone in my whole body."

"I'm sure that's not true," she said, hoping she didn't sound breathless. "There are tons of way to be creative." She looked up into his eyes. "You just haven't found yours yet."

"I guess not." He held her gaze, never looking away. Those eyes. The way he looked at her. It could make most women swoon. But technically he was her boss and she wasn't looking for a boyfriend, a lover or any unnecessary attachment.

She had started this little interlude with the intention of simply being friendly. But it was ending with her feeling more than just that.

"I should go now."

"You should. It's late."

"You should go home, too, Drayson."

"I will." He shut his laptop and stood. "Let me walk you to your car. I don't want you walking out there alone."

"I do it all the time without you, Chase."

"But now that I know your name, I wouldn't feel right about letting that happen. Especially if I knew there was something I could do to change it."

Whoa. This man. She might be headed for trouble.

Chapter 2

Chase sat outside on the patio of the little sushi place next to Sweetness Bakery. It was still a little too cool to sit outside and dine this early May day, but there he sat, sipping the warm tea the waiter had brought him and watching the foot traffic going in and out of Sweetness Bakery. He was running numbers in his head. For every three customers Lillian's had, they had five. Two-thirds of those customers took their purchases to go. One-third of those customers came out with large bakery boxes. It was too late in the day for people to bring doughnuts to work. Sweetness was selling a higher percentage of cakes and pies than they were.

"Spying on the competition, are we?"

He recognized the voice. It surprised him that he recognized it because he'd only had one conversation with her, but he looked up to see that petite, pretty female with the delicious smile and expressive eyes standing a few feet away from him. "Amber," he said, feeling the need to tease her. "Amber Bernard. You work in the bakery. As the barista. I remembered."

She grinned at him. "At least now I know I'm not forgettable."

No, she wasn't. In fact he'd thought about her all night after he walked her to her car. He kept picturing her face. The way she ate that cookie. The way she licked her lips and moaned filled him with a pure surge of lust that took him completely off guard. But it wasn't just that that kept him thinking about her. It was her smile. The way her face lit up when he told her about his last trip, the way she made him forget about work, when that was the only thing on his mind 99 percent of the time. "I'm not spying. Well, not really anyway. I'm just running numbers."

"You're running numbers while sitting outside and staring at our biggest competition? I'm just an artist so maybe I don't know how these things work."

"Come sit. I'll explain." She looked apprehensive for a moment.

"I don't think I can. I'm heading to the bakery now. I don't want to be late."

"You can't be late if you walk in with the boss. Sit down for a minute."

She walked over and he couldn't help but notice the way her hips swished in the long colorful skirt she was wearing. Her style would normally be a little too bohemian for his tastes, but on her it worked. On her, it was a combination of sexy and adorable that he had a hard time taking his eyes off of.

"Okay." She gave him a mischievous smile as she took the chair next to him. "You going to let me in on your evil plan now?"

"No evil plan here." He looked into her eyes as he said it. "Everything with me is always all good."

"I bet you say that to all the women you encounter."

"No. Only the special ones." He was flirting with her. He didn't mean to, but there was something about Amber that made him want to. Besides, she had started this. He was just minding his own business when she walked into his world.

He liked women, went on his fair share of dates. But all of the women he went out with were very much like him. Driven. They had practical careers with a tried-and-true path for growth. He figured he would marry a woman like that one day. Not a woman like Amber. Not that he was even interested in dating Amber, but he couldn't pass up the chance to engage in a little conversation with a woman whose eyes sparkled when she got excited and whose smile made a man feel funny on the inside. "Look at the consumers who are walking out of Sweetness. What do you notice?"

"Hmm." She placed her hand on her chin and leaned a little closer to him to get a better look. Her arm brushed his. And there it was again. That little rush that was more than attraction and felt a lot like lust. "Their clientele seems similar to ours. Not a lot of construction workers. Business people mixed with hipsters. People who wouldn't mind spending six bucks on a cup of coffee."

"Very good, Amber. What else?"

She smiled at his praise before she looked back at the door. "Most of them are taking things to go. I see a lot of large boxes."

"Excellent." He touched her arm, which was a mistake because she had the smoothest skin and it made him want to run his hand up her arm and down her body just to see if the rest of it felt as good. "I counted fifty-nine people walking into Sweetness in the past hour. At Lillian's we had thirty-five at the same hour yesterday. Our average customer is spending $5.19 when they visit. But just by watching them, I can see that a higher percentage of their customers are carrying out large cake and pie boxes. Their average customer is spending at least twice as much as ours. And while we have three times as many customers in the morning thanks to Mariah, their profits are still higher than ours."

"Wow. My head is spinning. You really are into numbers."

"It's my job. I spent a lot of time doing growth projections at my last job." He stood up and tossed money on the table to cover his bill. "Come on. I'll walk with you back to work."

They left the little restaurant and walked in the beautiful street toward the bakery. They couldn't have found a better location than the Denny Triangle section of Seattle. It was a mix of beautiful old houses and up-and-coming businesses. There was a park nearby. The perfect location to enjoy a sweet treat from Lillian's.

Chase had been a little apprehensive when he was approached with the idea of running a bakery. But now his chest filled with pride when he walked up and saw the beautiful storefront in this busy section of town.

"We talked about what I do for fun, but we never talked about what you do to let off steam."

"Oh, I BASE jump and skydive. There's this thing called parkour, which is like a military-style urban obstacle course."

"Really?"

"No." She laughed. "If it involves my feet leaving the ground, it's not happening. I love music festivals and traveling to beautiful historic places, but lately I've been focused on getting my degree and designing more jewelry. My dream—no, my *goal* is to get my jewelry into department stores one day. Everything I do is to get me one step closer to that goal. So it's work and grad school, and in my free time I design. Designing doesn't feel like work. It feels like…like…"

"Passion." He could tell she had a lot of it. He could only imagine the type of passion she would bring to bed. He had to shake off those thoughts. He wasn't supposed to be thinking about her that way. She was an employee after all.

"I do have passion for it. I can't think of anything else I'd rather spend a lifetime doing."

"It's good to have passion," he said as they walked up to the door. Chase always loved walking into the bakery and being greeted by the sugary smells and the feeling of hominess that enveloped him when he entered, but today he found himself not wanting to go inside.

It was a beautiful day in Seattle. The air was full of spring and for the first time he would rather blow off work and stay outside with this pretty girl than go to his office and bury his head in the books.

She was just so different from him. So much more interesting than the women he had dated recently. He barely knew her. He barely paid attention to the front-of-house employees, but he just wanted to talk to her some more. He wanted to know more about her.

"Are numbers your passion, Chase Drayson?"

"No," he said honestly, looking into her big brown eyes. He liked numbers. He liked working and investing, but they weren't his passion. He needed something he could be passionate about. "Maybe I'll let you know what it is one day."

He opened the door to let her in first. The bakery was busy. Not as busy at Sweetness had been, but they were doing pretty well so far and were on track to have a profitable first year, which was rare for new small businesses. Most of the time they only broke even if they made it to a year. He could see Mariah behind the counter, rearranging the stock. Jackson was there, too, chatting up some female customers, which was customary for him. But all of that kind of floated in the back of his mind because Amber was still in the front of it.

"One day? I'm not sure I can stand the suspense," she said with a smile that made him feel like smiling, too.

"I'm sure you can." He lifted her hand. She still wore the wire name bracelet, but she wore another one with it. It was also gold wire, but this one had three braided strands with white opals woven among them. "Did you make this, too?" He stroked his thumb over her pulse as he studied her creation. "It's so well done."

She nodded. "It's my birthstone."

"Do you think you could make me one?"

"I know you have a keen fashion sense, but I didn't think you wore beaded bracelets."

"I would like to send one to Lillian. Can you do this with pearls?"

"I can." She seemed surprised by his request. She shouldn't be. Chase knew good quality when he saw it.

"And one for Mariah, too. Her birthday is in—"

"I know when your sister's birthday is. I can make her one, too."

"Is five hundred enough to cover both the bracelets?"

"Five hundred dollars! That's way too much. I can't take that kind of money from you."

"Why not? That's what I'm willing to pay. Your work is good, Amber, and your time is worth something. Don't ever forget that."

"Mariah is my friend and I work for your family. It just doesn't feel right to take that kind of money from you. I can do it for the cost of the materials."

"Plus a hundred dollars. Think of me as an early investor. Roll your profit back into your business."

"Okay, Chase." They looked at each other for a long moment. He realized he still held on to her hand, but for the life of him, he couldn't force himself to let it go.

"I have to clock in."

"You do." He let her go. "Have a good shift."

"Thank you. I will. I'll see you later." She walked

away from him and he watched her go. Hips swaying all the way.

"Hey." His baby sister came over to him with a curious expression on her face.

"Hey."

"You walked in with Amber?"

"Yes, I met her on the street on my way back from an errand."

"Oh? That's all?"

"That's all."

"Really? You were holding her wrist."

Chase suppressed an eye roll. His sister had grown up into a beautiful, intelligent woman, but she was still his baby sister and sometimes she annoyed him the way she did when they were kids. "I was looking at her bracelet. I didn't know she was a jewelry designer."

"You were looking at her, too, Chase," she said in a lowered voice. "You were looking at her the way a man looks at a woman he's interested in, and you were touching her."

"I ran into her on the street. I walked in with her. I looked at her bracelet. None of those things are a crime, and I'm pretty sure that none of them were your concern last time I checked."

"What's going on?" Jackson strolled over. "Why does Chase look annoyed?"

"He walked in with Amber. I just wondered how that came to be," she said lightly.

"Amber, the cute little funky chick with the wild hair who makes coffee for us?"

"My *friend* Amber," Mariah corrected. "The hard-working grad student and jewelry designer who works here and is doing her best to succeed."

"Is there something you wanted to say to me, Mariah?" Chase felt more than annoyed at his sister at that moment. He was getting the strong feeling that she did not want him anywhere near her friend.

"No. It's just that Amber is not your type."

"And you have become an expert on what my type is?"

"Everyone knows your type, Chase," Jackson said. "The type of women who speak three foreign languages and have hefty investment portfolios. Beautiful, dull, boring-as-hell women."

"That is not true."

Jackson yawned widely to make his point and Chase wanted to knock him on his ass then.

"She's my friend, Chase. My first real friend since I moved back to Seattle, and I saw how you looked at her. I just wanted to know if there was something going on between you."

"Because I walked in with her and looked at her bracelet? Well, you should congratulate me, because after one chance meeting on the street, we've decided to get married and move to Bora Bora. Amber tells me the snorkeling there is the best in the world. Neither one of us has ever tried it, but hey. You only live once."

Mariah blinked at him. "Shut up, Chase."

"Nothing is going on, Mariah."

"I think you should go for it, Chase," Jackson said. "She's cute. She's the opposite of you. You'll have some fun with her. I'm in full support of you expanding your horizons and having a little fling."

Mariah let out a noise that sounded suspiciously like a growl. "Sometimes I wish I had sisters."

"No, you don't." Jackson set a loud smacking kiss on Mariah's cheek. "We're more fun."

"You're as fun as a hive of angry bees."

She left them then, leaving Chase with something to think about. Staying away from Amber might be a good idea. She did work for them and she was his sister's friend. And she had the potential to be distracting. With this business just starting, he needed to focus on growing it.

Something made him look over to the coffee café where Amber was already hard at work. She looked up at him and smiled, and Chase knew then that ignoring her was going to be a losing battle.

It was a battle he would be okay with losing.

"I'm going to head out for the night," Nita, another barista, said to Amber as she slung her bag over her shoulder. "Are you going to be okay with closing up alone?"

"Get home to that cute boyfriend of yours. I know he has been working nights lately."

"Thanks." Her eyes traveled over to the corner table in the café section. "Chase Drayson is here. If you hear something move, it's him. I was here a couple of nights ago and nearly jumped out of my skin. I thought the world's largest rat had broken in but thankfully it was just him."

Amber laughed. "Thanks for the warning. I won't make that mistake."

"I'm surprised he took the leave of absence from his job to work here. Salary-wise, I'm sure he made in one day there what he makes in two weeks here."

She hadn't thought much about it, but all the Draysons had taken a risk to work here. Jackson was somewhat of an entrepreneur and was used to taking risks like these. Mariah worked here because she wanted to escape the difficult past she had with her former husband. But Chase… She wasn't sure why he had taken this risk, yet she knew he loved his younger siblings. She could see it in the way they interacted. "Maybe blood is thicker than money, so to speak."

"I'm sure he's got enough of it to last him a lifetime already. A few years ago, a woman claimed she was pregnant with his baby in the hopes of cashing in. But that Mr. Drayson is one careful man. Of course the kid wasn't his. I'm not sure he ever slept with her, but that's the type of woman Chase attracts. Gold diggers. He's a quiet man, but not a weak one and he certainly isn't stupid. He knows what he's working with and he chooses his partners carefully, but I don't think he trusts easily. He goes for a very specific type of woman."

"Oh?"

"Yeah. Chase only goes for elegant, Ivy League–educated women from well-off families to avoid opportunists. He might have a little fling here and there, but no one ever knows about it. He seems like the kind of guy who should be married with two kids already, but I don't think he trusts anybody enough to let them get that close to him."

Amber nodded. It made sense. It made sense that he went for women who were the opposite of her. She usually stayed away from men like him. "How do you know so much about Chase?"

"He and his family are big in the Seattle society circles and so is my cousin, Simone, who used to date him. She always says he was the one who got away."

"Oh. Tell her I'm sorry for her loss."

"You're no sorrier than she is." She laughed. "I've got to go. I'll see you later."

She watched Nita walk out before she turned her attention back to Chase.

He was caught up in work again. Eyes glued to the screen, fingers on the keyboard. Forehead scrunched in concentration. She used to think that he was cold. Aloof. Maybe a little bit snobbish. But after talking to him a few times, she realized that he was none of those things.

What he was was incredibly focused.

And *fine*.

Amber was an artist so she could see beauty where others sometimes missed it, but no one could deny how handsome he was. How symmetrical his features were. How rich and deep the color of his skin was. She thought of chocolate diamonds when she thought of him. She loved her intricate wire pieces, but if she was going to design a piece of jewelry to represent him she would use chocolate diamonds and white diamonds swirled together in a beautiful necklace to be worn close to the heart. Something classic and elegant with a little bit of a twist.

It was no wonder he was a target for shady females. He looked like a man with a lot to offer.

She was staring at him this time, she realized as she wiped the same section of the counter for the dozenth time. He hadn't noticed she was there. Hadn't felt her eyes on him yet. She had noticed *him* at the sushi place. She hadn't meant to stop. Told herself to keep on walking by, but she couldn't go by without speaking to him, without having those gorgeous dark eyes of his focus on her. He pulled her in with those eyes. With that deep, smooth voice. He made her want to stay and talk and know more about him when she should have gone on and ignored him and stayed away from him.

He wasn't her type of guy. He had money. He practically smelled of money. That may be a positive with most women, but it wasn't for her. People with a lot of it didn't often realize how hard it was to get. He didn't bat a lash when he tossed a fifty-dollar bill on the table to cover a tab that couldn't have been more than ten. It nearly took her breath away, though. She had to work hours to make that much money.

And then when he asked her to make the bracelets, he offered her more than she could have imagined. And he did it all while telling her to value herself more.

No man had ever told her that. No one had ever told her that.

He was all wrong for her. Too rich. Too organized. Too buttoned-up. But she still couldn't force herself to stay away.

She turned back to her espresso machine and a few minutes later she once again slid a steaming drink in front of him along with a plate of shortbread cookies.

"You must have read my mind." He looked up at her as he lifted the cup.

"You needed a caffeine fix?"

"No. I was thinking I needed a beautiful woman to bring me my caffeine fix."

She tried to stay cool, but the line made her blush. "Oh. You're smooth, sir. I thought you could use a break."

"Please. Sit down." He smiled over his mug just before he took a long sip. She watched him drink the special coffee she had made just for him and watched his Adam's apple move as he swallowed. She wondered what it would be like to pop a button on his shirt and place her lips on his throat. She wondered how his skin would feel beneath her mouth. She wondered how he would smell. A clean scent. Or something a little darker, a little spicier. Either way she was sure it was intoxicating.

She mentally shook herself. *Where did that thought come from?*

She would stay far away from that neck. She didn't like to mix business with pleasure. She made it a rule. She needed this job. It was helping her pay her way through school. She couldn't afford a fling with her boss.

"Myers' coffee is always good, but you did something special to this," he said to her.

"Mexican coffee. My own special recipe with just a

hint of vanilla, cinnamon and chocolate. When I serve it at parties, I go all out and make it with tequila, Kahlúa and melted vanilla ice cream. But I toned it down for you tonight. This bakery doesn't have a liquor license."

"Do you throw a lot of parties?"

"Between working here, getting my master's and designing jewelry, I don't have time to throw any parties. The last one I threw was for my ex's thirty-fifth. I went through a lot for trouble for it, only to break up with him a month later. I'm kind of wishing I had broken it off before I bought him the most expensive thing I've ever purchased in my life."

"Don't tell me you bought him a car?"

"Do I look like the kind of woman that would go around buying men cars?"

"I don't know. Women do all sorts of things for the men they love."

He was right. She had been so much of her life leading with her heart. She had been prepared to give up a lot of things to please Steven, but in the end giving up herself seemed too big of a price to pay.

"What did you get him?"

"An original James Van Der Zee photograph. Do you know who he was?"

"A photographer. Famous for capturing the Harlem Renaissance through his lens."

"Exactly." She smiled at him, impressed that he knew who she was referring to. "I found a small photograph of his in a shop and thought my ex would love it. He didn't. He was hoping for a new camera, which would have cost even more than the photograph."

"Some men don't know how good they have it. You must have really loved him if you gave him such a gift."

"I thought he was the love of my life at one point. But I think I loved the potential of him." She'd bet her ex wouldn't say the same thing about her. He loved what she could do for him. He felt like he was a serious photo journalist, while she was just playing at her jewelry design. Jewelry making he called it. He referred to it as her hobby instead of her dream, treated it as it something that she merely liked instead of had a passion or talent for. She put up with a few years of slights and digs, with him diminishing what she did while lifting up his own work.

The truth was, they had been in the same places in their careers. He'd had one piece picked up by a national magazine the year before they met, but nothing big after. The only jobs he could get were for small local newspapers and unpaid gigs for bloggers. Amber's business had been growing at the time; she had designed some pieces for the wealthier set and gotten her work carried in a few small boutiques. And she had supported him, too. Picking up the slack by taking on extra shifts when his jobs had all but dried up at one point, but she stuck by him, a lot longer than she should have, because she had been in love then. She'd thought with her heart instead of her head. But that was all done now.

Chase seemed similar to her ex. Serious about his work. Focused. Driven. He was being nice to her now, ordering bracelets for the women in his family, but he probably thought her jewelry design was just a hobby, too. And one man in her life like that had been too many. She never wanted to experience that again. That's why finishing her degree and learning the business end was so important. She was ready to show the world and anyone who doubted her that she was a serious artist and that she had a lot to offer.

That's why she was adopting a no-men policy. Chase was incredibly good-looking, heart-poundingly so, but she was going to keep her distance. Some conversation. A shared plate of sweets was just enough.

Amber couldn't afford any entanglements in her life right now.

"What do you mean by that?" His eyes swept across her face, studying him. "Potential?"

"Everybody has potential," she said, remembering that she had said that about her ex. "Don't you think about a woman's potential before you decide whether you are going to date her or not? Her potential to be a good partner. Her potential to be a wife. Her potential to be a mother. Her potential to further her career. I'd bet you're the type of guy who has a spreadsheet with fifty-six characteristics a woman must have in order to date you. And each woman you meet is put into a column. Fling, casual partner or lifelong mate." She thought about what Nita just told her. Amber knew she was the exact opposite of the women Chase normally dated, but that was okay. She wasn't looking to be his potential partner and she didn't want him to think she wanted anything else from him either.

"You think you know me so well? First you think I'm boring and now you magically know what I want in a woman." He raised a brow at her and smiled. She found it incredibly sexy. There was a little dimple on his cheek. The urge to kiss it came over her. She wondered what he would do if she leaned over and kissed his face. How he would react? What would be his next step?

She shook her head, trying to shake off the feeling of wanting to kiss him for the second time that night.

"I just know you're organized. I saw the business plan you constructed for this place. I'm learning how to write them for school, but yours was incredible. Beautiful, really. I've never seen so many colorful charts in one place. And you say you're not artistic."

He took a long sip of his coffee as he looked at her. She felt like blushing with the way his eyes kept passing over her face. It was silly. She was an adult, but the way he looked at her made her feel like a girl again. "How did you see our business plan?"

"Your sister showed me. I was having trouble with an assignment and I asked for her help. She showed me your work. I was incredibly impressed, but I guess I shouldn't be. You went to one of the best business schools in the country. You're a pro at it."

He nodded. "I spent many years in the corporate world. If you ever need help with an assignment, you can come to me. I won't even charge you for my time."

"How sweet," she said, wanting to take him up on his offer but knowing it probably wasn't a smart idea. She was pushing the limits of her willpower by being here with him tonight. "I might take you up on that."

He nodded and reached for a cookie. "I still want to hear about this guy with potential that you bought the Van Der Zee for."

"He was a photographer. I met him while I was taking an art class at the local university. He was one of those people with big visions. He did what he called artistic photo journalism. Wanted to change the world with his work."

"That sounds admirable."

"It was, but the relationship was a little one-sided. And being with somebody who just takes can be draining. I felt like I was sacrificing what I wanted, so he could live out his dreams. I couldn't do that. I watched my mother do that. Give up her dreams to be a wife. To raise a family. I know she loved us. And not once did she treat us like we were a burden, but I knew she wished she could have lived out her dreams. She was an illustrator. A great one. Some of her work made it into magazines, but I think her dream was to do children's books."

"She gave it up completely? Was your father not encouraging?"

"He didn't discourage her, but there were four kids and my brother was always sick when he was younger. Life got in the way. Money needed to come in. My mother had no choice but to be practical. She sacrificed her dreams for us."

"And you don't want to be like her?"

She shook her head. "I want to have a career for her. I feel that there's always a little sadness in her. A little regret that she was never able to share her work with the world."

"You should encourage her to try again. Even if it doesn't get her anywhere, you should encourage her to draw again. Maybe take a class or two. I know a woman who gives scholarships to African American women over forty for school. I can recommend her for one."

His kindness took her by surprise. And it was then she knew he wasn't all that similar to her ex. Steven would have never thought about someone else's dreams, much less go out of his way to help them achieve them. "You would really do that?"

"I'll make the call tomorrow if you want." He took a card out of his pocket and wrote a phone number on the back. "My home number is on here. Talk to your mother. If she wants to go through with it, call me and I'll make it happen."

She picked up the card and studied it for a moment, studied the bold handwriting, the sleek design of the card, anything so she wouldn't have to look him in the eye. She was feeling a little more emotional than she would like. She was feeling as though she really wanted to kiss him. "I'm sure she would love to go back to school. She'll be grateful." She looked up at him only to find him already looking at her, those beautiful intelligent eyes sweeping across her face. "I'm grateful for this."

"I admire creative people. You may think I'm all about numbers, but I'm a big believer in dreams. This bakery is here all because Lillian had a vision and a dream. There's nothing wrong with a little dreaming."

"That's sweet, Chase." She was sitting in the chair next to him and leaned over and kissed his cheek. She hadn't meant to. It was unconscious, really, but her lips sought out his face. They lingered on his smooth skin, just a moment too long. He smelled good. Clean. Expensive. With a little bit of the heavenly scent of the bakery lingering on him.

She lifted her lips away, tried to back away before she got caught up, before she wasn't able to make herself back away. But it was already too late. Because Chase slid his hand along her cheek and brought her face closer to his.

He kissed her. Not hot and fiery like she might have wanted, but slow and deep like she needed. That kiss gave her another glimpse inside of him. It told her how he might be as her lover, in her bed. He would take his time just like he was taking his time now, kissing her thoroughly, not leaving any part of her mouth untasted. He would do that to her body and she could just see him starting at her toes and working his way up. His lips caressing her calves, her thighs, in between her legs.

She moaned, arousal spiking even though it was just a soft kiss, even though he probably hadn't meant for it to be so sexual. But she was that attracted to him. "You deserved more than what that guy gave you," he said softly as he lifted his lips from hers. "I'm glad you realized that."

He sat up straight then, drained his coffee mug and shut his laptop, as if nothing had happened, as though he hadn't just kissed the hell out of her. "It's getting late. Let me walk you to your car."

Chapter 3

"Why didn't you tell me you had gotten a new television?" Jackson said to Chase the next evening as he spread his long legs out on Chase's leather couch and stared up at his new forty-two-inch LCD. "It's so beautiful I think I might cry."

Chase just shook his head as he watched his younger brother make himself comfortable while he made them both pre-dinner drinks at his bar. "Maybe I didn't think you would care that much, or maybe I thought if I didn't tell you I could avoid your putting your dirty feet all over my furniture."

"I was going to suggest we try that new fusion place down the block." Jackson kicked off his shoes. "But the game is on and it would just seem like a crime to leave this big beautiful screen alone all night."

"We don't have to go out." He handed Jack his dirty Martini, kind of relieved that his brother wanted to stay in tonight. He was feeling a little funky today. His sister had noticed, but he told Mariah he thought it was allergies or an oncoming cold that was making him feel off. It was neither of those things, though. It was Amber.

He had kissed her last night. He wasn't planning to. He hadn't meant to, but she leaned in and kissed his cheek. Her smooth full lips, her warm sweet breath caressed his cheek, her lovely feminine smell flipped on a switch or something inside of him and made him forget about logic and common sense and all the rules he had set up for himself when it came to women, But he had to kiss her last night. He couldn't stop himself and he was glad he hadn't, because he knew if he'd walked out of there without touching his lips to hers, he would have regretted it.

She hadn't kissed him back. She didn't pull away, but she let herself be kissed. Opened her mouth beneath his, went soft and pliant from his touch and made little breathy moans while he explored her mouth, driving him wild. And it was right then he knew he couldn't just kiss her and walk away. He knew that one kiss wouldn't be enough and that he would have to have more.

Mariah hadn't explicitly said anything to him yet about not seeing Amber, but he knew his sister didn't want him messing with her friend. She was right. Starting things up with an employee of the bakery would be inadvisable. It could end up messy and Chase didn't do messy. Especially after that woman, with whom he had done nothing but kiss, showed up, claiming that she was pregnant by him. He knew it was wiser to stick to his checklist. Stick to a certain type of woman. A woman who was just like him, but those lips… One kiss, one taste wouldn't be enough to satisfy him. He wanted to kiss her all over. He wanted to start at the top and work his way down. He wanted to kiss every inch of that supple brown skin and bury himself inside and feel her legs wrapped around him.

His attraction to her was real. It was intense.

He couldn't get her off his mind all last night. He was that attracted to her and it was powerful, but it was stupid. Maybe he had been too cautious lately. Maybe he had gone too long without sex, without the touch of an attractive woman. He went out with some beautiful, financially independent, incredibly intelligent women, but none of them made his blood pump. None of them inspired vivid fantasies.

Amber had. After just one kiss. Hot and heavy relationships usually burned out fast and ended badly. He didn't want to risk that. He had fallen asleep determined to put her out of his mind.

He woke up today hoping to have forgotten about that kiss, about wanting her, but all day at Lillian's he'd unconsciously kept looking for her, hoping to get a glimpse of her every time he left his office, hoping to hear her voice, but he didn't, because she hadn't worked today.

It was probably a good thing. He needed his space from the beautiful woman, whose smile he couldn't take his eyes away from and whose words had him wanting to hear more from her.

"Chase!" Jackson's voice permeated his fog.

"Yes?"

"What did you want to eat?" He had his phone out probably scrolling through the listings on his restaurant delivery app. "Chinese? Italian? Burgers? I'm voting for the Spanish place on Lake Street. They deliver and I'm in the mood for paella."

"That's fine. Whatever you want."

"Whatever I want?" Jackson sat up and looked at him. "Are you okay? You never give in that easily. We usually have a debate ending up in a compromise, if I don't give in."

"I like paella. No argument."

"Uh-huh." Jackson nodded slowly. "Mariah was right. You must be getting sick."

"Me being agreeable means I must be sick? What if I just happen to agree with you? Spanish food sounds good."

"I think so. You'll let me order whatever I want off the menu and you'll eat it?"

"You can order every dish they serve as long as you pay for it. Oh, and use a coaster. My coffee table is too nice to be messed up because your glass is sweating all over it."

"That's more like the Chase I know." He slid a coaster beneath his glass. "I was wondering when you were going to notice that. If you got your furniture from the store like everybody else you wouldn't care so much about your precious table. But no, you've got to get a turn-of-the-century, reclaimed-wood table with an accent."

"What?"

"This is foreign, isn't it?"

"Yeah. It went with my furniture and I like nice things. I work hard to make money so I can afford nice things. What's wrong with that?"

"Nothing, but that's where we differ. Money is to be made and lost. Gambles with huge risks make huge gains."

"You do things your way and I'll do things mine, and we'll see where we both end up." Jackson lived his life so differently than Chase. He dated everyone he wanted. He flirted wildly, not giving a damn about the consequences or how things might end. But things were rarely messy for his younger brother. Women loved him. Hell, everyone loved him. He was friends with everyone—exes, even competitors. No one could seem to stay mad at him. Chase often wished he was more like him. More easygoing. But he couldn't be. He just wasn't wired that way.

His landline rang and he got up from his chair to answer it. "Hello?"

"Hello, Chase? It's Amber."

"Amber." He was surprised to hear her voice. "How are you?"

"I'm fine. Very fine actually."

Chase had to bite his tongue to keep from saying *yes, you are.*

"I'm calling to tell you that I spoke to my mother and she would love to take some classes and would be grateful for any assistance you can offer."

"Why do you sound so formal, Amber? I thought we were old friends by now."

"Old friends?" He could hear the smile in her voice

and wished he was with her to see it. "Who you calling old?"

"That's better. I'll call my friend and set up the scholarship process. Have your mother look for some classes that she wants to take and let me know."

"I will." She was quiet for a moment. "Thank you, Chase. This means so much to both of us."

"Don't mention it. Are you working tomorrow?"

"Yes."

"I'll see you tomorrow then."

"Yes. You will."

They disconnected, Chase feeling a little bit of a rush after talking to her.

"Amber?" Jackson walked over to him. "You were talking to that fine barista?"

Chase was busted but he didn't feel the need to lie to his brother. "I was."

Jackson had a slight knowing grin on his face. "I'm sure she's not contacting you at home because she's calling in sick or changing her shift."

"No. She wasn't."

"And since you aren't kicking me out right now, I'm assuming she wasn't calling to tell you that she was coming over?"

"No. She's not coming over." He was slightly disappointed as he said those words. He could just imagine the way she would look standing at his front door, asking him if she could stay the night. And again he wondered what the hell was wrong with him. He barely knew her and yet he wanted her with a growing hunger.

"Will you stop being so damn evasive. I want you to get with this girl. Maybe she'll loosen your tight ass up."

"It's not what you think. You know how Kenya Ashworth offers scholarships for adults going back to school? I'm setting one up for Amber's mother."

"You mean the scholarships that you donate a large sum of money to every year?"

"Yes."

"So you're paying for her mom to go back to school. You must have it bad for this girl. Why don't you just take her to a fancy restaurant and buy her something shiny. It might be easier."

"I'm not paying for her to go back to school. The scholarship fund is, and I believe in education. Not everyone grew up with the opportunities that we've had. It's important for me to give back."

"Yeah, giving back to a woman with a behind like that makes it a little easier, doesn't it?"

Chase shook his head as he grinned at his brother. He couldn't help but agree with the man.

Amber's heart was beating a little harder than she would have liked after she hung up the phone.

Chase.

His deep, smooth voice. The way it rolled over her. Amber was never one who liked to be read to, but she had the strange desire for Chase to read to her so she could close her eyes and get lost in his deep voice. She could imagine what it would feel like to lie in bed with him, her head on his hard chest, his warmth surrounding her along with his intoxicating smell while he read to her.

She got all tingly just thinking about it. She shouldn't be getting all tingly. She shouldn't be thinking about him like that at all, but she couldn't help it.

"Was that him, sweetheart?"

Her mother came out of her kitchen with tea and toasted peanut butter and marshmallow sandwiches for both of them, bringing back memories of her childhood. Her mother was always serving them, bringing them something, making sure they were all okay. Even now that they were all adults. Amber couldn't remember a time when she had seen her mother do something for herself. "Yes, Mama. It was. You're all set up. You just have to pick your classes."

"I'm so excited!" She set down the tray and hugged Amber. "I haven't been in school in over thirty years. I hope I can keep up."

"You will, Mama." They sat down at the kitchen table and Amber studied her mother, a former activist turned stay-at-home mother of four. She was still beautiful well into her late fifties with shockingly white hair and pretty coffee-colored skin. "You're one of the smartest women I know. I'm sure you'll be the best student in there."

"You're such a good girl to do this for me, Amber. I had no idea you knew I wanted to draw again."

"I saw you pick up a book about becoming an illustrator while we were in the bookstore. I always wondered why you had given up your dream."

"It was a different time. When I had babies women

stayed home. They raised their families. They spent their lives making sure their children's happiness came first."

"I feel guilty that you had to sacrifice your happiness for ours."

"Why? I don't regret a moment of it. All four of my children have made it through college. All of them are happy and healthy and doing well. As a mother I feel a tremendous sense of accomplishment, and tonight I feel especially proud that my daughter was thoughtful enough to make it possible for me to go back to school."

"I didn't do much. My friend…" She shook her head. "I guess he's more of my boss… He's the one who is making this happen."

"You said friend first, Amber. Tell me about him."

"Chase?" She thought for a moment, trying to figure out the right words to describe him. "He's Mariah's brother. You remember Mariah, don't you?"

"Yes, she's a lovely girl. Chase must be a very handsome boy."

Amber nodded, but she didn't think there was anything boyish about the man. "Chase is very good-looking but doesn't seem to realize how handsome he is. He's a little on the conservative side. He was in corporate finance for a long time before he and his siblings decided to open Lillian's of Seattle."

"What else about him?"

"He loves his family. He's thoughtful. He's intelligent. He makes me smile," she said thinking about him. "I don't know him that well. Those are just my impressions of him."

"I might have believed that if you hadn't added in that 'makes you smile' part. Your father made me smile. I would spend hours after I left him grinning ear to ear like a total ninny, but it felt good to smile like that. Being with him was just so easy. Is that what it's like with Chase?"

It was easy to be with Chase. Easy to get caught up in his conversation. Easy to lose her head just looking at him. "He's good man."

"You should invite him over for dinner. Make him something special. I think your shrimp and cheesy grits is probably one of the best things I have ever tasted."

"You want to have a little dinner party to thank him?"

"No, sweetheart. I think my presence there might interfere with your love connection."

"Mama!"

"What? Your friend might be on the conservative side, but I'm not. How do you think you got here?" She touched Amber's hand. "Listen. You haven't dated anyone since Steven, who frankly made you cry more than he made you smile and who I never liked anyway."

"You didn't like him?" she asked, shocked. "You never told me."

"No. I didn't want to cause any tension between us. And I didn't want to drive you any closer to him. The man was a self-centered, pompous ass. His pictures weren't changing the world, and if he wanted to make a statement he could have helped out his community. He could have volunteered at the food pantry. He could have shot a couple of weddings to help out when finances were tight, but all he did was complain and put you down about your dreams. I don't think this Chase fellow is like that. Didn't you mention something about him asking you to create a couple of pieces for him?"

"Yes, but I think he's just being nice. Most people think my jewelry design is a cute little hobby."

"But not him. If he thinks your old mom should go back to school, then I think he'll be on board with whatever you choose to do."

"You don't even know him. Hell, I barely know him. Why are you fighting for a relationship that doesn't even exist?"

"You could get to know him. You've shut down every man who is even mildly interested in you. What happened to my joyful baby girl who always led with her heart?"

"That baby girl got her heart stepped on by a man who told her it was her job to unconditionally support him because that's what good women do for their men. I really believed that for a while. It took me a long time to realize he was stealing big parts of me."

"When did you realize that?"

"Remember that piece I was working on for Janna's wedding?"

"That lovely flowered hair comb with the blue stones? Your sister adores that piece. Her something new and something blue. She still wears it when she goes someplace special."

"Yes. It's an intricate piece that took me a long time. I thought Steven would understand why it was so important to me, but two days before the wedding he wanted me to drop what I was doing and go to his friend's opening at an art gallery. When I told him I couldn't, he got upset with me. He told me I could work on my little hobby whenever I wanted, but his friend only had one opening. I tried to explain how important it was to me, but he told me that the only things that should be important to me were the things that were important to him. And it was if he threw cold water on me and I woke up. I kicked him out then."

"You should have smacked him."

Amber smiled at her normally nonviolent mother's aggressive statement. "I wanted to. Looking back on that time, I realize that he was jealous. My pieces had gotten picked up in five boutiques then and he hadn't gotten a job in a month. He was bitter about having to teach a photography class at a local community college while I was making money doing what I loved. I was understanding at first, but it got to the point where his negativity was sucking the life out of me."

"You're too wonderful to be stuck with a man who doesn't appreciate you."

"I figured that out a little too late."

"But you shouldn't punish Chase for it."

"He hasn't asked me out. And I work for him and you know I don't like mixing business with pleasure."

"Fine. Don't date him if you're uncomfortable with it, but it has been nearly two years since Steven and I'm concerned that you're afraid of risking your heart again."

Amber didn't say anything, but her mother was right. She was afraid of risking her heart again.

* * *

"I want to welcome you all here," Mariah said, looking at Amber, Jackson and Chase once they were all gathered in Chase's office the next afternoon.

Amber thought Mariah looked very serious and very beautiful for someone who spent the majority of her day baking. Today she wore a formfitting gray pencil skirt, a silk cream top and sky-high gray suede heels. Not the image that came to mind when one thought of a baker, but even though Mariah's looks might've been deceiving, no one should've been fooled. The girl knew how to throw down in the kitchen. The Draysons had used a lot of the recipes from the Chicago bakery here, but Mariah would not settle for being a copy of the original. She wanted to provide baked goods that no one else was selling anywhere else.

"Why are you welcoming us here? To my office," Chase said from his seat on the couch next to Amber.

Amber had never been in Chase's office before, never seen inside of it because the door was mostly kept closed. It was small but very nicely decorated with a small couch and a desk that looked as if it was made of mahogany. There was a large painting on the back wall that at first looked like an ordinary seascape, but on closer inspection Amber realized that she recognized the painting.

"Is that a Palmer Hayden?" she blurted out.

Chase sat up and looked her in the eye. She was sandwiched between him and Jackson, but she barely noticed Jackson's body next to hers; it was Chase's that she felt. His firm thigh pressed against hers, his bare forearm, brushing against her arm. His smell. His clean, expensive, intoxicating smell infecting her. "You know Palmer Hayden?"

"He was a Harlem Renaissance–era painter most famous for his John Henry series. Of course I know about Palmer Hayden. I'm surprised you do."

"Chase loves all that fancy, bougie crap. You should see his apartment. It's like a museum in there," Jackson said.

"Isn't that the pot calling the kettle bougie, Mr. Food Snob whose favorite foods are things most people can't pronounce?" Chase countered.

"Don't start, you two," Mariah said with a sigh. "I wanted you here so we could have a taste test."

"You called us in here for a taste test?" Jackson sucked his teeth. "I thought it was something important you wanted to talk about, like finances or the Bite of Seattle."

"Mariah wouldn't call a meeting about finances. I would call one, and we should talk about Bite of Seattle. We really have to nail down our plan. I have been researching the most successful exhibits from previous years."

"Of course you have," Jackson said. "I'm surprised we don't have a ten-page report in our hands yet."

"It's coming," Chase answered.

"What is this Bite of Seattle thing anyway?" Amber asked. "I've heard about it for years, but I've never known what goes on there."

"Bite of Seattle is a three-day food festival that takes place every July," Chase explained, looking at her again.

Her mind almost wandered away from his words because she was so caught up in how good he looked today in his lightweight baby blue sweater, which looked beautiful against his rich brown skin. His sleeves were pushed up, showing off his strong forearms. She had never seen much of his skin before because he always wore long-sleeved button-down shirts. But today his arms were on display and she had to admit they looked very powerful for a man who had spent his entire career working behind a desk. "This is the first year Lillian's will be taking part in it. And since Sweetness Bakery has dominated the pastry market there for the past few years, it's important that Lillian's makes a strong showing."

"Lillian is coming out for it," Jackson continued. "We need to show the community that we make the best product. There are cooking demonstrations, wine and food sampling. It's the opportunity to bring in a wider variety of consumers."

"Which is why I called you all in here for a taste test," Mariah said.

"Yes," Everett, Mariah's new fiancé and Amber's former boss, walked in just then. Amber saw Mariah's heart jump into her eyes. She was in love with Everett and he was just as crazy about her. He walked over to his future bride and softly kissed her on the mouth, not caring if her entire family witnessed it.

Everett was a young widower raising a son alone. Mariah, with her good heart, was just the woman he needed to open his heart to love again.

"Mariah has been bouncing recipe ideas off us for

days now. I don't think I have tasted so many odd concoctions in my life."

"You liked my potato chip cookies."

"I did. I like everything you do because you are brilliant."

"This is why I'm marrying the man." Mariah grinned at her future husband. "But I called you here so that you can taste these." She picked up the small covered tray she had placed on Chase's cabinet and removed the top with a flourish. On the tray were small, perfectly decorated cupcakes that looked as if they could be consumed in one bite.

"You're including me in this?" Amber asked her, surprised to be included with the family.

"Yes." Mariah nodded. "We've become tight. You're important to me. I wanted to have the people most important to me here when I revealed my cupcake bites."

"Thank you," Amber said, feeling honored. "Those are adorable."

"They look good, but I need you to taste them. If the flavors aren't perfect, we can't have them at the Bite of Seattle. So I need for these to be perfect. I call this one cherry cordial. It's chocolate cake with a cherry filling, chocolate mousse icing and a chocolate-dipped cherry on top."

"Wow." Jackson sat up and studied the creations closely. "My teeth hurt just looking at them."

"Just try one and tell me what you think. Be honest. No sparing my feelings."

"We've been your brothers all your life," Chase said, reaching for one. "I think you should know us well enough to know that we would never spare your feelings."

Mariah grinned at him and handed out the tiny cupcakes. Amber bit down into it and an explosion of flavor filled her mouth. There was no other way she could describe it. The rich chocolate, the slightly tart cherry filling, the creamy mousse. Amber had been around some great baked goods in her time as a barista, but Mariah had something special. She must have inherited it from Lillian.

"Damn, Amber," Jackson said. "We should put you in commercials for the bakery. The way you eat a cupcake will make people come running to Lillian's just to try one."

"What?" she asked, feeling slightly self-conscious.

"You look blissful," Chase said in that smooth voice that she loved to hear. "I agree with Jack. I think men would line up just to watch you eat." He looked back to his sister. "The cupcake is a winner Mariah. We'll debut it at the Bite of Seattle. I'm sure it will be a hit."

"Great." She looked at him and then back at Amber with a suspicious look on her face. "This is the only solid recipe I have so far. I would like you and Jackson to come up with something, as well. Three Drayson siblings—three cupcake bites. All premiering at the festival in a couple of months."

"I want mine to have bacon in it." Jackson stood up and walked toward the door. "Bacon and bourbon cupcakes. There'll be a line down the block to get those."

Chase shook his head. "What do you think, Everett? Will you be able to stand the next two months of

Mariah trying out a hundred new recipes? Because I know my brother will come up with the craziest thing he can think of, and Mariah will try to accomplish it."

"I can take it." Everett grinned back. "But I really came to take her out to lunch before we have to get EJ from school."

"I would love to go to lunch." She took his hand. "Remember, Chase, come up with something good for your bite. Think outside the box. I know that can be hard for you sometimes."

"I'll try my best, sister dearest," he said drily.

"You want to walk out with us, Amber? I know your shift is ending soon."

"Oh, no thanks. I've got to talk to Chase for a moment."

"Do you?" Mariah raised her brow.

"I do." She smiled at Mariah's not-so-subtle attempt to figure out why she wanted to speak to Chase.

"Okay." Mariah sighed. "Call me later."

"I will." She waved at them and then turned her attention to Chase.

"They're gone," Chase said, standing up to close his office door. "Has my sister grilled you about us yet?"

"No," Amber said, swallowing. They were in his office alone. Away from everyone else's view but not safe from everyone's gossip. It wasn't even that she cared about that kind of crap. She was more concerned about herself, about her irrational, insane attraction to him. She wasn't sure she could trust herself around him. "Why? Has she grilled you?"

"She saw us walking in together the other day." He

sat down beside her again, close to her even though he didn't have to. "I guess I picked up your hand to study your bracelet and that made my sister very curious."

"She hasn't said anything to me. We haven't really gotten the chance to talk lately. I know she has been busy with Everett and EJ."

Chase nodded. "She's always wanted a family of her own. And now with Everett she's found it. I think she'll be a great mother."

"A mom who loves to bake is a pretty amazing thing to have."

"Did your mother bake a lot when you were a kid?"

"No. She was a big fan of dessert though. She made banana pudding on the last Sunday of every month because that's when my grandmother would come visit us for dinner. And she made this really incredible chocolate parfait thing with chocolate graham cracker crumbs, chocolate sandwich cookies and fresh whipped cream. And in the summer she would make a dessert called tangerine cream that was cool and tangy and tasted like summer. My mouth waters just thinking about it."

He leaned forward and kissed her very gently, his hand sliding up her cheek. She shut her eyes and kissed him back. Last time she had let it happen, last time she had just experienced it. But not this time. She wanted to kiss him back and taste his lips and participate in this beautiful thing. He lifted his lips, his eyes sweeping across her face before he leaned in to kiss her once more.

It was a much shorter kiss this time, but she still felt it through her entire body. "The way you described your grandmother's tangerine cream… It seemed like you were there at a picnic table, eating it. I wanted to see if I could taste it."

"You're full of crap. You just wanted to kiss me."

"That's true." He grinned at her. "But the way you talked about it made me want to kiss you."

"You shouldn't kiss me like that, Chase."

"I know, but I can't help it. You're very beautiful. All I can think about is kissing you."

"Oh?" She hadn't expected him to be so honest with her. If she were honest with him, she would tell him that she couldn't stop thinking about him, too. Thinking about kissing him and touching him. But thinking about talking to him, too, getting to know him more. "Why do you think you shouldn't kiss me?"

"Because you work here and we both know better than to get involved."

"We do." She nodded. Chase was cautious. He was smart. He needed a woman like him so that he could marry her and have children who were elegant and ordered just like him.

"But—" he leaned closer and kissed along her jawline "—just because we know better doesn't mean we're going to do better."

"Quit it. We're in here with the door closed." She shut her eyes as his lips traveled up to that little spot behind her ear that made her knees go weak. She was trying to keep her train of thought but it was hard. "People are going to wonder what we're up to."

"I don't give a damn what they are wondering," he

said into her ear, his breath brushing across her skin, making her nipples tighten painfully.

"Stop anyway. I wanted to talk to you about something else."

He removed his lips from her and she mourned their loss for a moment, but she hadn't come here for this. She did have a legitimate reason to stay behind after the others had gone.

"What is it?" His eyes searched her face in that way that they always did, the way that made her feel self-conscious.

"Why do you look at me like that?"

"Because I find you incredibly beautiful."

She blinked at him, not knowing what to say, but she did feel beautiful when he looked at her. He made her feel as though there was no one else on earth, just the two of them in their private little bubble. Her mother wanted her to follow her heart and most of the time she did, but with Chase it could lead to heartbreak and she didn't have time for that right now. "I finished the bracelets you wanted." She slipped them out of her apron pocket and handed them to him.

He studied them for a while, turning them over in his hand, paying attention to every detail. She had to hand it to him—he really did seem interested in her work. Very unlike her ex, but she couldn't tell if he was truly interested in what she did or if he was trying to get in her pants.

Part of her didn't care. She thought a night in bed with Chase might be...incredibly satisfying.

"This is excellent work. It's hard for me to grasp the fact that you made them."

"You don't think a girl who makes coffee can be an artisan?"

"Not that." He looked into her eyes. "It's hard for me to grasp the fact that anyone can take a grain of an idea and make it bloom into something beautiful like this. Mariah can dream up exotic flavors and Jackson can come up with all these great business ventures, but I can only see things in black and white. Things that are straightforward. I need projections and charts and evidence that things will work out. But you can wake up and think 'I'm going to make something beautiful,' and here it is."

She wanted to kiss him again. She wanted to reach over, grab his collar and pull him into another long, slow, hot kiss.

But she didn't because his kisses were bound to be a danger to her mental health. "You have something amazing inside of you, Chase. I know you do."

He nodded as if he didn't believe her. "These are really beautiful. Let me pay you what we originally talked about. These are worth it."

"I won't let you pay me for those. You're helping my mother with her dream. This is the least I can do for you."

"It's very important for me to give you something for these. I won't feel right if you don't allow me to pay you for your work."

"Okay." She stood up, needing some space from him

before she kissed him again and really got herself in trouble. "But not now. I have to go to class."

He took her hand, squeezed her fingers as he looked into her eyes, and she was once again tempted to throw her common sense out the window. "I'm not going to let this go, you know."

"I know. But you have to let me go," she said as she slipped her hand from his and walked out of the room.

Chapter 4

Chase went back to his desk, prepared to return to work. Only he couldn't. He couldn't focus on compiling his report for Bite of Seattle or coming up with cupcake flavors or analyzing yesterday's receipts.

Amber.

He had kissed her again. Kissed her pouty, soft-looking mouth when he told himself that he was going to keep his distance from her, stay away, ignore her altogether to lessen his fixation on her. But that plan had gone out the window when Mariah called the meeting in his office and sat Amber next to him on his small couch. Doing that was like telling him that she wanted them together. Amber smelled slightly of caramel today. He knew she used it a lot in her coffee drinks. The scent of it stayed on her skin and gave Chase the strong urge to lick it off her.

But he resisted, settling for her arm brushing his and her leg pressed against his thigh. He noticed that she leaned more toward him than Jackson, that she looked him in the eye when she spoke to him, never breaking contact. He'd thought there was something there between them, that it was not just one-sided and he'd known for sure the moment he kissed her and she kissed him back. It wasn't the kind of kiss you gave somebody new, but a kiss you gave somebody you had known for a long time. The kind of kiss that excited you because you knew what was coming next and it was always so damn good.

There was an email from Mariah waiting when he finally turned his attention back to his computer. She must have sent it before she got to the car. He laughed. The subject line of her email told him exactly what was on her mind.

What are you up to? In your office alone with Amber?

Chase thought about ignoring the email because his love life was really none of his sister's business. But he didn't.

THERE IS NOTHING GOING ON.

A moment later there was a reply from his sister.

Then why did she want to speak to you alone?

He replied again.

It's none of your business.

Not ten seconds later there was another reply from Mariah.

Amber is not the kind of girl you have a fling with.

It was true. She definitely wasn't. He wasn't looking for a relationship. He wasn't even looking for a date. And yet he had kissed her. And yet he wanted more. And yet he knew that he wouldn't be satisfied until he had her. He was going to try to resist her. Chase Drayson was a man who had never failed at anything in his life, but he knew that this time he might.

Amber tried to hide her yawn as another customer walked up to the counter. She hadn't gotten home till almost eleven last night. She'd had a late class and a few of her classmates had stayed after for a little while to study for the big final they were having next week. It was important that she do well on this final. She was having a bit of trouble in this class and hadn't done as well on some of the assignments as she had hoped. She wasn't in danger of failing. She would be damned if she let that happen, but she wanted to do well, wanted to keep her grades as high as possible, just to prove that the jewelry designer with the wild curly hair had a brain in her head and knew her stuff.

"Hello. What can I get for you on this fine spring

day?" she said to the customer who appeared to be somewhere in her seventies.

"Oh, there is so much to choose from, I just don't know what to get."

"Well, maybe I can narrow it down for you." Amber stepped from behind the counter and looked at the menu with the woman.

"Hot or cold?"

"You have cold things here?"

"Yes, ma'am. We have a beautiful peach green-tea lemonade and six other flavors of tea. I could make you an iced coffee if you would like."

"Iced coffee? I've never had that before. That might be something I try when it gets a little warmer. Let's go with hot coffee today."

"Okay. You sure you want coffee? I can brew you a lovely cup of tea."

"Yes, coffee. I like to have tea in the morning."

"Well, I suggest you come back in the morning, too, because Myers does tea as well as coffee. Do you like a bolder dark roast or something a little milder?"

"Milder, please. It'll be better for my reflux."

"Now we're getting somewhere. Would you like something plain or a little fancy?"

"Fancy?"

"Yes, ma'am. You'd be surprised to know what I can do with a cup of coffee."

"We'll go fancy then."

"Last question. Do you like your coffee sweet?"

"My daughter likes to say I have a bit of coffee with my milk and sugar."

"You're my kind of girl." Amber smiled at her. "I know just the thing for you." A few minutes later she presented the woman with a beautiful mug of coffee topped with whipped cream and drizzled with chocolate syrup.

"That's a work of art. What it is?"

"I like to call it 'So Sue Me.' It a light roast coffee with a mix of white chocolate and tiramisu syrup with whipped cream and a chocolate drizzle on top."

"Thank you, honey." She took a bill out of her wallet. "I think I'll enjoy this."

"If you don't, let me know and I'll fix you something you do."

She watched the woman walk away, feeling good about the transaction. Her job wasn't just about serving good coffee. It was about good customer service, too. She knew how it put a damper on her day whenever she received bad service. She didn't want anyone else to have their day affected negatively because she was tired.

"I know you are planning to hit it big with your jewelry business, but even if you make millions of dollars a year, could you stay on as our barista?" Mariah rested her head on Amber's shoulder for a moment. "You're the best one we have."

"Thank you. When I was a little girl, I dreamed of one day making fine coffee drinks in one of the best bakeries in Seattle."

"No, you didn't." Mariah grinned at her. "None of us dreamed of being here. I wanted to be married to a wealthy prince and live on a tropical island."

"Everett may not be actual royalty, but he could buy you a big house on a tropical island."

"Maybe a vacation home. I like being around my family again. I didn't realize how much I missed them when I lived in Chicago. Besides, you and I just became good friends, how could I move away?"

"If your beachfront mansion has a guesthouse, I would be more than happy to stay with you for extended periods of time. I could design jewelry out by the pool and sell my wares to the tourists."

"You imagine big, don't you?"

"I do."

They grinned at each other.

"It's a nice dream," Mariah said with a sigh, and that reminded Amber of what Chase had said about dreams a few days ago.

"We haven't talked in a while. We should catch up."

Mariah's eyes lit up. "Is there anything new we need to catch up about?"

"No. You don't have to look so excited. I just haven't seen you in a while."

She looked slightly disappointed. "Oh, I thought there might be a new man in your life."

"No. Nobody but Professor Habibi."

"Is he a sexy academic type with a six-pack?"

"He's an eighty-year-old with a hearing aid."

"Oh." She frowned. "You would tell me if something was going on, right? I told you about Everett."

"Yes, Mariah. I'm not seeing anyone. I promise." Chase had asked if Mariah had grilled her about them yet. She guessed that this was it. They had kissed a couple of times, but she wasn't seeing him. They definitely weren't dating.

"We should all have dinner. Jackson was talking about trying this new Chinese place that just opened. I'll invite Chase. We'll make it a night."

"Okay. That sounds fun—just let me know when."

"I'll call you later. I've got a meeting with a supplier in a few minutes, but we'll definitely set something up for next week."

"Sounds good."

Mariah squeezed her arm before she walked away. Amber attended to a few more customers, but it was the time of day when the coffee café slowed down. She wished it wasn't. She needed the customers, the little bits of conversation to keep her going. She was tired, feeling a little run-down these past couple of days. She needed to stay busy so she could get through the next part of her day.

Chase walked behind the counter and poured hot water into a paper cup and dipped a passion fruit tea bag in there. She was surprised when she saw him pour honey in the cup. She hadn't pegged him for a tea drinker.

"I think you could use this." He handed the cup to her. "You look tired."

She was touched by the simple gesture. "Is it that obvious?"

"Not with the customers, but I can see it in your face. You should go to bed early tonight."

The words *you should come with me* almost slipped off her tongue, but she caught herself. The vivid image of climbing into bed with him and sleeping in his arms appeared in her mind. She could just imagine how the skin of his hard chest would feel against her cheek, how his arms would feel wrapped around her, how languid she would feel after hours and hours of lovemaking.

She was aroused, she discovered. Unexpectedly and fully aroused just by thinking about him, just by standing before him. She had never experienced this kind of attraction to a man.

"Are you all right, Amber?" Chase lifted his hand to her cheek, stroking the backs of his fingers along it. He glanced at the clock and issued an order to the busboy who was wiping down the tables to take over the counter.

"Your shift is almost over." He grabbed her arm. "Come sit down."

"I'm fine, Chase."

"You're exhausted. You're sitting down." He led her to the back of the café to the table with the comfy armchairs in the corner where he sometimes liked to sit when he worked. He had kissed her for the first time at this table. She mentally shook her head again. She couldn't believe that she was holding that memory in her head. She certainly couldn't remember where her ex had kissed her the first time. But she remembered Chase's kiss and what he was wearing and how he smelled.

And what it felt like. She would never forget what it felt like or how she'd stayed up all night thinking about his lips on hers. Thinking about how much she would love to feel them on hers again.

"Drink your tea."

"Chase, I'm fine. I swear."

"You looked like you were going to pass out."

"I wasn't. I was just thinking about some stuff."

"Okay," he said, clearly not believing her. He walked away from her then, only to return with a large gooey chocolate chip cookie for her. "Eat this. It will make your blood sugar go up."

"But—"

"No arguments. Just eat it."

She did as he asked and he watched her chew the cookie. It was a damn good cookie. One of the bakery's bestsellers. She allowed herself to have one a week. They were large, and she knew if she ate more than one, her behind would end up spreading from here to California. "You eat some, too." She broke off a piece and held it up to his mouth. He looked her in the eye while she fed it to him and she realized what she was doing. She was feeding the man she worked for, in the place she worked, in the middle of the day. Luckily no one was around them and they couldn't easily be seen from the counter.

"Why are you so tried? What were you doing last night?"

"Nothing fun. What did you do last night?"

"I went to the gym, took a shower and watched three hours of wrestling."

"What?" She let out a startled laugh. "Wrestling, like gold-medal, men-in-singlets wrestling?"

"Get real. I'm talking pile driver and chokeslam wrestling."

"I don't believe you." Super educated, corporate finance guru, Chase would never watch a tables, ladders and chairs match.

"I'll show you my cable bill. I order every event on pay-per-view."

"Why?"

"It's ridiculous and fake and absurd, but I like it. It helps me unwind."

She smiled at the thought of it. "What does your family think of this?"

"They don't. They don't know anything about it. It's my dirty little secret and now I'm sharing it with you."

"I'm honored." She liked having that little secret with him. She liked that she knew something that nobody else knew about him. She liked that he wasn't as stuffy as the world thought he was. "I used to watch it myself when I was a kid. I had a thing for that big, sexy, Samoan guy."

"He's an action star now."

"Really? I don't keep up with many movies."

"Because you don't have time. You accused me of not taking time to enjoy life and yet you're running yourself ragged. When is the last time you relaxed?"

"What day is it?"

"Thursday."

"Oh, then it was eighteen months ago."

He smiled, showing off those gorgeous white teeth of his, and she smiled back, unable to help herself. "That's not the answer I wanted to hear."

"I'm a busy woman. I thought a man like you would appreciate that."

"I do. Come out with me."

She blinked at him. He had kissed her twice. His request shouldn't have been a surprise and yet it was. She felt kind of breathless hearing it.

"Let me buy you lunch. Wherever you want to go."

Yes. She wanted to say yes, but her mouth wasn't working for some reason. "What time is it?" came from her mouth instead.

"It's two thirty."

"Two thirty!" She jumped out of her chair and pulled her coffee-scented work shirt off to reveal a cream-colored tank top that she loved to wear with her paisley-print maxi skirt. "I can't have lunch with you. I have to go."

"Where do you have to go?"

"To class. I teach a class every Thursday. I'm going to be late."

She stepped away from him, prepared to sprint out the door, but something made her look back. "Thanks for the tea and cookie. I appreciate it."

He simply nodded and she rushed away from him to the back to get her things and clock out. She was out of breath by the time she left the bakery and she couldn't tell if it was because she was really in that much of a hurry to get to class, or if she was in that much of a hurry to get away from Chase. She wanted to go out with him, to be alone with him, but she didn't trust herself around him. It would be far too easy to give in to temptation, to let a few kisses turn into full-blown lovemaking. And maybe a little bit of lovemaking was what she needed. She hadn't been with anyone in a long time. She hadn't felt the touch of a man in over a year. Chase was right. She was tense. She did need to relax.

A night with Chase would certainly help with that, but then she would have to come to work in the morning and see him and know what he felt like inside her, know what his face looked like when he made love, know what sounds he made while he was taking his pleasure.

And that was bad because she worked for him. She was good friends with his sister. She didn't want to risk either thing.

Her car was parked just around the corner from the bakery and she could feel her heart rate slow down as she approached it. She loved her old red VW Bug. It had been a gift from her grandfather on her sixteenth birthday. He and her father had restored it for her and she'd had it ever since. She got in and put the key in the ignition to start the car, only the car never started. It sputtered and died.

Shit, she cursed to herself. How much was this going to cost her?

Chapter 5

Chase sat at the corner table for a few minutes after Amber rushed out. He had been turned down for dates before, but he never had a woman run away from him after he asked. If he didn't know any better, he could have sworn he had seen smoke where she had stood. She had left the room that fast.

A barista. A jewelry designer. And now a teacher. The last one he was surprised about. He wasn't sure how she had time to do it all and do it well. Of course, she could be using it as an excuse not to go out with him. Though, he wasn't sure why she would. She seemed to enjoy his kisses. She seemed to like kissing him back. He thought that they had a connection. He had felt it. But maybe he was wrong. Maybe he was slipping. He wasn't a player, but he never had trouble getting a woman. But Amber, it seemed, wasn't going to be easy to get.

He shouldn't have asked her out. He hadn't meant to do it then, like that.

But the question just slipped from his lips. He thought she was beautiful and vivacious. She made his insides heat every time she smiled at him. And every time she bit into something sweet and shut her eyes, letting out one of those deep moans, a pure surge of lust traveled straight to his groin.

But did they have long-term potential?

Did they have a single thing in common?

A shared interest?

She was just so different from him in every way. Different upbringing. Different background and careers and educations, but he liked her anyway.

He liked her and he thought about being with her despite everything.

But backing off was probably for the best. Getting involved with somebody in the workplace could be messy and awkward. If he wanted a little noncommittal bit of fun he could turn elsewhere.

Amber didn't seem like a no-strings-attached kind of girl.

He got up and mentally shook himself as he walked back to his office. He should take her refusal as a sign to move on.

Should.

Didn't mean he was going to.

Not two seconds after he sat down behind his desk, his sister appeared inside of his doorway.

"You heading out for the day?" he asked, noticing her keys and bag in hand.

"I'm going to meet with a supplier. We're going to talk chocolate."

"Sounds exciting." Mariah didn't move. "Was there something you wanted, sister dear?"

She frowned slightly, and he knew she didn't like it when he called her that. "I saw you talking to Amber. Is there something you want to tell me?"

"No." He folded his hands and just stared at her.

"I saw you touch her face."

"Did you see me make her sit down? You talked to her just before I did. You couldn't tell she was exhausted?"

"You saw me talking to her?" she asked.

"Of course I did. You don't think I'm aware that everyone can see what I do, what we do in this bakery? Do you think if I was carrying on with Amber, that I would be so open about it in front of all our employees?"

"I—I... Why did she want to talk to you alone yesterday?"

Chase inhaled deeply and opened his desk drawer where he pulled out the bracelet that Amber made for Mariah. "Happy early birthday. Don't stand there. Come and get it."

"Oh." She took the bracelet from him and looked at it. "Oh." She looked back to him. "I love it. Amber made this?"

"I had one made for Lillian, too." He pulled that one out of his desk and handed it to her, too.

"Gorgeous." She looked up at him kind of surprised. "She'll love it. This was very thoughtful of you."

"I know. I still haven't paid for them yet, so you'll probably see me talking to her again. I like Amber, Mariah. As a person. She manages the café section. You're going to see me talking to her again. I'm going to be friendly with her. I might even touch her again. I do not want, need or appreciate your giving me the fifth degree every time you see us together."

"She's been mistreated before. She's been hurt. I know you. I know you're a good man, but if things go wrong, I don't want to lose her as a friend."

"Why would you lose her?"

"Because you're my brother and in the end I have to stick with you."

"Why are you so sure I would hurt her?"

"You wouldn't mean to. But you have been burned before. You both have and you have thrown up these walls protecting yourselves from getting close to anyone. I'm not sure how two people so wounded and unwilling to open their hearts could ever make things work."

"I'm not wounded."

"A woman accused you of fathering her child and then dumping her. That would leave a mark on anyone."

He thought about that difficult few months in his life. Two dates. He had been on two dates with a woman and nearly eight months later she showed up at his place of work claiming that he had fathered her child. If he had, he would have taken care of his responsibilities, welcomed a child. But he knew he hadn't. Because he had never gone to bed with her. He would be a fool not to recognize the similarities between Amber and that woman. She was a cocktail waitress working her way through school. Beautiful, outgoing, likable. Someone he might have gone to bed with. Someone who had invited him in, but he hadn't slept with her. There was something in his mind that had warned him not to take things all the way, even when things had gotten hot and heavy.

He still ended up paying for going even that far.

"I'm recovered."

"Amber needs to be supported. She needs to be loved completely. And after what she went through with that guy, she deserves it."

That last line stuck with him. It must have been her ex. The one she threw the big party for, the man she must have spent a substantial amount of her savings on to buy that old photograph for.

The one who didn't appreciate her.

He was a damn fool, her ex.

Amber deserved to be appreciated, treated like a queen. But was Chase the man to do it? He didn't know. Maybe she had turned him down because she wanted to be with someone more like herself. Someone artsy and creative. Someone not as rigidly focused as him. He could come up with business plans and projection charts in his sleep, but the thought of coming up with a cupcake flavor for Lillian's debut at the Bite of Seattle was making him sweat.

"Okay, Mariah."

"Just okay?"

"Yes, just okay."

She nodded. "I have to get going right now. But I want all of us to go out to dinner next week. Including Amber. Will you come?"

"I will."

"Good. We have to let Jackson pick."

"I know. He knows the best places. The best chefs. He thinks he's the best at picking out restaurants."

"He is, though."

"I know, but as the oldest, I believe it is my duty to give him a hard time."

She smiled at him. "I'll set things up, Chase."

"Let me know how things go with the supplier."

She nodded at him and was off.

He opened up his laptop again, ready to get back to work. Ready to push Amber and all the conflicting thoughts he had about her out of his head.

"Um, Chase?"

He looked up from his computer to see her there. And for a moment he believed his thoughts were magic. But then he noticed the distressed look on her face. "What's wrong?" He stood up. He knew she was exhausted. He shouldn't have let her walk out the door earlier.

"I hate to ask you this, and normally I never would, but I'm in a bind. My car is dead. Will you please take me to my class? Mariah pulled away just before I could get her attention."

"Of course." He grabbed his keys. "Why do you hate asking?"

"I don't like to ask you for favors."

"Why not?"

"Because I don't want you to think I want anything from you."

He stopped her, placing his hand on her shoulder. "Not even my friendship?"

"I'm broke, Chase. I've got student loan debt up to my ears and a business that nobody thinks I'm going to make successful. If people see a girl like me anywhere around you, they are going to think I'm a gold digger and I'm hanging around with you to get ahead. Plus I work for you, so I don't want any of the other employees to think that I'm getting special favors."

"Whoa." He put his hands up. "I think you're wrong about that. We've got good people working here. And even if they did think that, who gives a damn what anybody thinks?"

She frowned, seeming frustrated. "Maybe I just don't want *you* to think that."

"I don't." It was true. He hadn't thought that about her at all, not really. And the fact that she thought that people might spoke volumes about her.

"I…" She trailed off. "I would like to be your friend. A real friend, Chase. Do you think we can try that?"

There was something there between them, a need. A pull. Just something that neither one of them could deny. Staying away from her would be too hard. He could be her friend. He wanted to be her friend, to get to know her, to be around her. "We can try that. But then don't be afraid to ask me for a ride when your car is dead and stop worrying about what anybody thinks of you."

"I normally don't. It's just that I'm used to doing things for myself. I've had to do things for myself."

"Trust me, I'm not looking to save you. All I wanted to do was buy you lunch."

"But you keep kissing me."

"You keep looking like you need to be kissed."

"What makes you think that?"

"Fine. You can kiss me first next time. And you can buy me lunch if it makes you feel better. Lobster, if you really want to feel empowered."

She grinned at him. "The most you'll get out of me is two-for-one vegan hot dogs down at the food truck on the corner."

"Vegan hot dogs? You're vegan?"

"No. Love me a big slab of ribs, but the hot dogs are cheap and they'll fill you up. Especially if you put loads of mustard on them." She glanced down at her watch with its woven wire band. "I really do have to go. I'm going to be late for class."

"Okay, just tell me where to go and I'll get you there."

A few minutes later he pulled up in front of a community center in a part of Seattle he had never seen before. It wasn't as upscale as the area where Lillian's was. Nor did it have the cozy feel of the community center in his old neighborhood, but this was where Amber taught.

"In the mornings there are classes for seniors and moms who are at home with their kids and are looking for something to do. But the afternoons are all about the afterschool program," Amber said, reading his mind. "A lot of these kids will end up involved in some things that they have no business being involved in, so the leaders here try to provide programming that will appeal to a lot of the preteen and teenage population. There are cooking classes, video game design and music production. My class is jewelry design, and I helped create a curriculum that empowers young girls to express themselves creatively."

"I'm impressed."

Amber smiled at him. "Maybe you should come teach here. You can call it 'miniature moguls.' Your sister told me about all your business ventures when you were a kid. She told me that you made enough from them to buy your first car brand-new when you were seventeen."

"I'm good with money and numbers. I don't know how I would fare with kids."

"Give yourself more credit, Chase." She leaned over and kissed his cheek. "Thanks for the ride. You got me here in record time."

"I'll walk you up." He was sure she would be fine. She had been fine without him for who knows how long, but he didn't feel right leaving her just yet.

"You don't have to."

"Let me scope out the place. My family loves to give back. Maybe we can see about giving back here."

"Okay." She nodded and then stepped out of the car. As they entered the building, he could see that the inside of the building was vastly different from the outside. There was a large mural lining the walls. The Seattle landscape, done in bright vibrant colors that sucked the viewer into it. He spotted kids in the painting. Children sitting on buses and peeking out of windows. Children laughing as they played in the street.

"It's something, isn't it?" Amber asked him, seeming to have slipped inside of his head.

"I can't take my eyes off it."

"A student's father painted it. Actually, I should say he designed it with some of our high schoolers. He taught a ten-week class where they worked on the mural from start to finish. He would love to do other community spaces, but he hasn't been able to manage it with his work schedule. Since he got his second job, he doesn't have the time to stop by."

"You mean he doesn't paint full-time?"

"Painting doesn't pay the bills as well as landscaping does. He's had to pick up waiting tables because his youngest girl needs braces."

"Talent like that and waiting tables. It's a shame."

"He's got five kids. He's doing what he has to do."

They walked down the hall filled with framed papers. Chase could see everything from typed essays to kindergarten counting assignments. They all were graded. All had a positive message on them.

"That's our wall of achievement," Amber said. "There's no grade requirement to get your work up there. It just has to be something the kids worked hard on in school and feel proud of. Some kids work damn hard for Cs and we want to celebrate them."

"I like that idea. It builds them up."

"We work hard on that. We want to give kids positive self-images so they go out and do good things in the world."

"You should be a spokesperson for this place. I'm sure the donors would come rolling in."

"Donors are great so we can offer more, but what we need most is people to volunteer their time. We have young men who need mentors and girls who need to know that they can be good at science and math."

He nodded. So many people he knew would rather write a check than really get involved—he was trying to think of anyone he might know who would be willing to give some of their time.

"We're here." Amber opened the door and Chase saw that there was a group of preteen girls already waiting for her there.

"Hello, ladies!" She smiled brightly at them, as if she was truly happy to be with them. "You're all here early so I guess that means you're ready to get right to work today."

"We are, Ms. Bernard," one of the girls said as her eyes traveled to Chase. "But we want to know who that man is. You told us you didn't have a boyfriend."

"I don't, Tisha. And if I did, I'm not sure that would be any of your business."

"Oh, Miss—" the girl grinned "—you know you would tell us. We're your girls. And that guy is very cute."

Chase grinned. He could tell that Amber was slightly embarrassed, but she played it cool. He should have taken that as his cue to leave, but he really wanted to see how she handled the girls' inquisitiveness.

"This is my friend, Mr. Drayson. He is not my boyfriend because boys have cooties and I don't like them."

"Miss Amber!" some of the girls groaned.

"But seriously, he owns the bakery I work in. He

just wanted to see where I teach. He didn't believe me when I told him that I willingly spend my free time with you all."

"A bakery? Did you make cupcakes for us?" Another girl asked him.

"I just keep track of the finances," he told them. "I've never baked anything in my life."

"You should take a class," one of the girls called out. "They have a baking class here, but I think they don't let old people in."

"Old. You hear that, Amber? She just called me old."

"Don't be too hurt by it. They think anyone over thirty is ancient. Of course I escaped that fate, only being twenty-eight."

"Don't laugh. Old age will sneak up on you before you know it and you'll be searching for your dentures and using a cane like me."

"I can't wait. I'll be saying things like *whippersnappers* and *malarkey*. And eating dinner at four thirty."

"Miss Amber, stop playing." One of the girls giggled.

"You're right. No more playing. We're here to work and learn how to make some fabulous things." She went to the locked closet in the front of the classroom and began pulling out small kits. "Does anyone want to tell Mr. Drayson what we have been working on?"

To his surprise everyone's hand flew up.

"Libby."

"We are starting a small business."

"Seriously?" He looked at Amber who nodded.

"We're calling it Brainy Beauties That Bead," Libby went on to explain. "It's separated into three departments. Home decor, jewelry and key chains. We're diversifying."

"Diversifying?" he asked, kind of blown away that a bunch of twelve-year-olds knew what they were talking about.

"Yes," another girl spoke up. "Diversifying means branching out into new business opportunities, not just expanding your business. We started out just by making earrings and bracelets, but not everyone wants or needs jewelry and we were completely ignoring the male market."

"The male market?"

"Yup, there's a whole bunch of hippie granola guys in Seattle. Miss Amber said the right word for them is *hipsters*, but those guys wear beaded bracelets and necklaces, too. We made them in wood tones—black, brown and gray."

"Impressive," Chase said, meaning it. "You sound serious. I'm going to let you get to work." He waved to Amber. "I'll see you later."

"Thanks, Chase. I appreciate it."

Amber walked out of the community center a little before six. It had cooled down a lot since she'd walked in and she was regretting not carrying her sweater with her. She had left it in her car, and then she remembered that she had left her car where she had parked it this morning when she had gone to work, and that her car was dead. Again. And that she had put more money into it than a new car would have cost.

There was nobody she could blame but herself for

this, and she wasn't going to let this little inconvenience of not knowing how she was going to get home tonight bring her down. She'd had a great class with the girls today. They were like little sponges, sucking everything in. She was glad she had gotten them past the point of just wanting to make pretty things. She hoped she was teaching them that pretty things could make you money, that running your own business could make you feel good. That it was possible for them to run a large company one day instead of just working for one.

She opened her bag and pulled out her phone, checking to see which bus route would get her home.

"You ready to go, Amber?" Chase walked up to her with two cups in his hand. To say she was surprised to see him was an understatement.

"What are you doing here?" she blurted out.

"I was waiting for you."

"Oh. I'm sorry. I didn't mean for you to wait. I feel terrible."

"Why? You don't have a car, and I'm done with work for the day."

"It's true. I had forgotten that I didn't have a car, but I don't want to take up any more of your time. You always seem so busy."

"I am, but that's because I keep myself busy. I took a leave of absence from my job, but I still do some work for them on the side."

"To keep your skills sharp."

"And to keep one foot in the door. I'm not sure how long I'll stay with the bakery. It was important for me to be involved in the first few months to make sure things got going smoothly."

"I wondered why you had gone into it."

"It seemed very important to Mariah. And Jackson. Jackson needs a direction."

"You don't want them to know you take care of them, but you do."

"Don't tell them." He flashed her a quick smile. "Now can you do me a favor?"

"I think I owe you one."

"Let me take you to dinner."

She paused for a moment, thinking of half a dozen reasons she shouldn't go, and one reason she should. Because she just wasn't ready to say goodbye to him yet. "Take me to dinner."

"Do you like jambalaya?"

"I do."

"Good. I know a place."

The place turned out not to be too far from the afterschool program in one of Seattle's newly revitalized neighborhoods. It was a small hole-in-the-wall called Little Nola's, and when she walked in she felt as if she was transported to New Orleans but in another time period. It was dimly lit and the walls were splashed with bright colors and bold paintings. The tables were made out of reclaimed wood and it all kind of had a '50s vibe to it. That combined with the heavenly smells of the food made Amber fall hard for the place.

"Chase." The bartender finished pouring a drink and came over to greet them. He was an incredibly handsome man, wearing a newsboy cap, jeans and gray vest over his well-fitting white shirt. "Glad to see you, my man."

"It's nice to see you, too, Eddie. How have you been?"

"Not as good as you, I see." He looked at Amber. "You brought a beautiful lady with you. You never bring women here. Hello, goddess. I'm Edward James Wallingford the Second. It's a pleasure to meet you."

"I'm Amber." She smiled back at him. The man was charming. She liked him immediately.

"Eddie owns this place," Chase explained. "We used to work together until he decided to open Little Nola's."

"Was in danger of having a stroke at thirty. I couldn't live my life that way. Screw the money, I needed happiness."

"Amen," Amber said in agreement.

"You two sit anywhere you want. I'll bring you out something spectacular."

"Where do you want to sit, Amber?" Chase placed his hand on the small of her back as they looked around the nearly empty restaurant. The heat of his fingers seeped through her shirt and she immediately grew warm all over, forgetting about the chill she had felt when she first stepped outside that evening.

"You've been here before, you let me know which seat is the best in the house."

"How about over there?" He pointed to a corner that had a huge painting of magnolias in bloom. It was one of the softer paintings decorating the place, making that corner of the restaurant seem cozy.

They headed to the round booth, getting in on opposite sides and somehow ending up together in the middle, their bodies touching. It was as if they were magnetized, as if some force was pulling them together. She wanted to pull away, but she couldn't. The attraction was too strong.

"This is the part of the evening where we both silently, awkwardly look at our menus," Chase said softly as he looked at her. "And try to figure out what the hell we are going to talk about. Only there are no menus to study. Eddie will bring us whatever he thinks is good."

She looked over to him, knowing he had nailed how she was feeling. There was tension between them. More heightened than usual, because for once they were completely alone outside of the bakery, away from anyone who saw them daily. Right now she didn't feel like the barista/manager who worked for his family. Or the woman who was friends with his sister. She felt like just a woman out with a man that she wanted to get to know. It had been a long time since she was just a woman out with a man.

"Is that what your dates are normally like?"

"I usually go out with women who are good conversationalists, but there is always that semi-awkward moment when you're both wondering how the evening will turn out."

"Are you wondering how the evening will turn out now?"

"I'm wondering if you think this is a date."

She opened her mouth then shut it, searching for the right words to say.

"Okay, ya'll." Eddie returned with a tray in his hands,

preventing Amber from saying whatever it was she had been about to say. "I fixed you a batch of my very special drinks made with my super secret, super special liqueur, some sweet-and-sour mix, some of our fresh squeezed lemonade and club soda for some fizz." He sat the drinks on the table. "And for your first course I have brought you our world famous boudin balls. You're not a vegetarian, are you?" he asked Amber as he set the items on the table.

"No, I'm a vegan and I'm morally against this pork stuffed ball you've placed in front of me."

She watched Eddie's eyes widen and she laughed. "I'm joking." She picked one up and bit into it. "Mmm." She closed her eyes as she chewed. Hot, deep fried, peppery and flavored with a spice she couldn't identify. "My grandfather used to make these when he came up to visit us. Don't tell him, but I think these are better." She opened her eyes to see two men staring at her.

"Where did you find this woman, Chase?"

"None of your damn business."

"She eats free. You come back here anytime you want, Amber." He took a step back. "I'll be back soon with your next course."

"Why does everyone always look at me when I eat something? Am I that bad?"

"Yes. And if I could, I would be with you every time you ate so I could see you close your eyes and moan when the first bite hits your tongue."

The way he said those words in his deep, soft voice caused a pleasant sensation to run all through her body. It was almost as though he was stroking her. She wasn't one who got turned on very easily—she never thought of herself as that sexual—but all it took was a few words from Chase Drayson and she became a puddle of hot liquid.

"You're going to make me self-conscious about eating around people."

"Why? A woman who enjoys food enjoys life. And you are beautiful. You shouldn't be self-conscious about that."

"Stop flirting with me, Drayson."

"I'm not. I don't flirt. I'm just telling you the truth."

"You don't flirt, do you? I see your brother walking around the bakery with that little swagger of his. Flirting with all the women who walk in there no matter what their age. I can't help but think he's full of it. But in a good way. Does that make sense?"

"Yes. That's Jackson. Loved by the masses."

"My oldest brother is like that. He's a pilot. He's based out of San Francisco now. Women just fall all over themselves around him and he eats every single bit of it up. He used to be an air force pilot, but now he flies commercially and looks damn good in his uniform."

"Is he married?"

"No. My mother prays every night for him to find a woman to settle down with, but he's not ready yet and he's not the type to break hearts. He only wants to have fun and I don't blame him. Our parents got married and had us young. We saw how much of their lives they missed out on because they had so much responsibility. Perry's going to do every wild thing he wants to do before he settles down and he's unapologetic about it. I respect him for that."

"Are you close with him?"

"I barely see him. He flies internationally mostly, but when we do get together, we have a great time."

"What about your other siblings. I think I remember you saying you were one of four."

"I am. Two boys. Two girls. I'm the baby. My sister's wedding was the last time we were all together. We rented a place up in Spokane just before it. It was important to my sister that we all have that time together. She said that it was the last time it was going to be just the four of us as we were. She made us relive our childhood. We played cards and stayed up watching horror movies all night and cartoons in the morning with huge bowls of sugary cereal." She smiled at the memory. "My brothers balked at first, but they went along with it because that's the kind of men they are and they ended up having a good time."

"It's good that you all are close."

"You're close with your siblings, too."

He nodded. "I feel like Mariah has always been a little closer to Jackson. He's more easygoing. I think she thinks I'm too stuffy."

"She wouldn't say that if she knew about your secret wrestling addiction." Amber grinned at him, still surprised by his admission.

"I'm going to keep that a secret. We can't let people know too much about me."

"Why not? What would be the harm in letting people know that you're human, that you watch something purely for entertainment's sake? That just like millions of other people, you find enjoyment in watching one two-hundred-fifty-pound man body slam another?"

"Same reason you go around letting everyone think you're a free-spirited wild child when you're really a workaholic in a flowy skirt."

"I am not a workaholic! You take that back."

"You have three jobs and you're going to graduate school. You work harder than anyone I know."

"I like to work," she said feeling slightly defensive.

"I know. You're just like me."

"Am not."

"You value education. You come from a large traditional family and you like to work. We're similar. I proved my point. Maybe I'm a little more adventurous than you." He looked her directly in the eye then. "When I play, I play hard."

She let out a slow breath, knowing there was a world of meaning in those words. The word *play* caused all sorts of images to fill her head. Him playfully kissing her, him playfully nipping the inside of her thigh, him playfully tumbling her into bed before he slid inside of her. She could play hard, too, and he was somebody that she would like to play with. "What if I played a little too hard before?"

She had played fast and loose with her heart. She had given it to a man who didn't love her the way she loved him, and she regretted it. She had been too softhearted, too easygoing, too go-with-the-flow. She had promised herself when she ended things with Steven that she was never going to be like that again, but then there was

Chase who she was so attracted to, who she wanted to be around all the time, who she thought about when her mind was supposed to be on other things, more important things like her career. He was dangerous. He was the type of guy she could really lose her heart over. The type of guy she could fall in love with, and it was crazy because she barely knew him and there were a million reasons that they were all wrong for each other. But that didn't change the way she felt when he looked at her.

"What did he do to you, Amber?" He took her hand in his and stroked his thumb along her knuckles.

"Nothing big. He just tried to strip the soul out of me."

Eddie returned then with a basket of bread that was still steaming from the oven. "I almost forgot to give you these. We make the best yeast rolls in the city. You should consider selling them in your bakery." He surveyed the contents of the table. "Why aren't you eating or drinking? You find hair in your glasses or something?"

"No. We were just talking," Chase said. "Sometimes everything else just kinds of fades away when we do."

Chapter 6

Their conversation had turned to other topics after Eddie had come to their table for the second time. Chase made an effort to keep things light, to make Amber smile. He knew people had bad breakups and feelings were hurt, but Amber's ex must have really done a number on her. It couldn't have just been that things went bad, that he was simply an ass. It was more than that because the look in her eyes when she spoke about him... There was true hurt there, deep hurt there and it made Chase want to soothe it away. It made Chase want to make her forget every shitty thing that the guy had ever done to her.

Those feelings surprised him. Alarmed him. He thought she was cute. He liked her smile, liked to talk to her. But soothe her?

She made him want to throw out his checklist, throw out the rules he had set up for a woman he was going to date because the rules didn't matter. Amber seemed the opposite of him on the outside, but they were similar creatures. And the more he learned about her, the more he wanted to know.

He pulled up in front of her building later that evening. It was a huge Victorian that was split into separate apartments. Even in the dim evening light Chase could see that it was painstakingly maintained, and all the original details of the facade had been restored. He hadn't been inside it yet, but he knew he liked Amber's place. She could have chosen to live in one of the hundreds of tall apartment buildings downtown, but she had chosen this place, in a purely residential neighborhood, away from the restaurants and the nightlife most young people her age sought. It seemed as though a person could find peace here after they came home from a long day at work.

"I want to invite you inside, Chase," she said without looking at him. "But I don't want you to think that this is an invitation for sex. I just want you to come inside my home for a little while."

"Okay, Amber," he replied, because there was nothing in that moment that he wanted to see more than the place she laid her head at night.

They stepped out of the car and he followed her closely up to her apartment. It was getting dark and he kept thinking about how often she must return home late at night. Alone, late at night. He didn't like to think of her alone out in the city after dark and now that he knew her better, he knew he would think about her on nights she had late classes, wondering if she'd gotten home okay.

"You're too quiet," she said as she turned the key in the lock. "What are you thinking?"

"That it's chilly and if I touched your arm I would probably feel goose bumps."

She paused and turned to look at him. There was something in her eyes, an emotion that he couldn't identify. "Come in, Chase."

Her apartment looked different than he expected. The major pieces of furniture were basic. A big comfortable-looking couch, a large chaise longue, end tables that she might have bought at any big-box store, but it was the little things, the little touches, that made her apartment homey. Her walls were covered with photographs. Mostly of her family. Black-and-white photos of her with her siblings, a large portrait of her parents embracing each other on the shore of the beach. She and a baby girl laughing.

There were also little framed photos of the places she had been. Hot air ballooning in the Oregon wine country. A beautiful shot of a waterfall that he recognized from Olallie State Park.

There was an enormous bookshelf on the far wall that had been stripped down and hand painted. The word *read* was painted in large bold letters across the side and there were tiny printed words covering the rest of the surface. "Dictionary pages," she said.

"You always seem to read my mind." He looked over at her. "I like it very much."

"Thank you. My sister and I made it." He nodded, not surprised that she'd made it herself. He looked further around the room. There were colorful throw pillows and blankets, mosaic vases filled with wildflowers and an old brick fireplace where the only painting in the room was.

Nothing in the room matched, but everything went together. It should have been jarring. There were so many things to look at and yet he felt relaxed there. It was so different from his apartment, which was luxurious and neutral and could pass for a very comfortable hotel suite.

"I'm not sure why I'm holding my breath all worried about what you think. I usually don't care what anybody thinks of my place because I love it. But I can see the wheels turning in your head."

"It fits you. I like you, Amber, and I like your place. Where do you design your jewelry?"

"Come." She grabbed his hand. He was sure she didn't mean to cause a jolt of electricity to go through him when she locked her fingers with his, but she did. He had touched her before. He had kissed her, but having her fingers intertwined with his seemed more intimate. More personal. It was closer than he had been to anyone in a very long time.

She led him to a small bedroom that was just a little bigger than a closet. There were built-in shelves on the walls with her tools neatly organized and on display and a narrow desk for a workspace with sets of clear plastic drawers that held her supplies. "Why is there a bed in here?"

"For the nights when I'm too tired to head down the hall to my room."

"I don't like that. I don't like that you're so tired you can't walk ten feet to your room."

"I have to work. I have to teach. I have to go to grad school. These aren't wants for me. I need to do all those things."

"You need someone to take care of you."

"I don't." She shook her head, her face set in a stubborn expression. "I can do it all. Do you think I'm not strong enough to handle it all?"

"I think you can, but we all need someone sometimes. There's no shame in that. There's no shame in asking for help when you need it."

She nodded. "Right now I need you to sit on the couch with me and watch TV."

"Only if I get to hold the remote."

"I'll let you hold it if you promise me no team sports."

"Damn. There was a synchronized swimming competition I really wanted to see."

"But I really need to see the world champion spelling bee. I've got money riding on the girl from Des Moines taking the whole thing."

They grinned at each other for a moment and even though he felt comfortable with her, he felt nervous. Nervous that he wouldn't be able to keep his hands off her, nervous that if he pulled her into a kiss like he wanted to, he wouldn't be satisfied until they were both naked and sweaty. And once he got her like that, he knew that just once would not be enough.

So he just took her hand again and led her out to her living room where they sat and watched reruns of *Law & Order*.

She had butterflies. That was the only way Amber could describe what she was feeling. Chase was sitting next to her, shoes off, arm wrapped around her, watching television as if this was something normal. As if it was something they did every night. It wasn't. And right now she could be designing jewelry or studying her textbook or making notes for next week's class, but she didn't want to do any of that. Tonight she was allowing herself to do nothing, to sit with a handsome man and relax. Only she couldn't relax fully because she had her feet tucked beneath her and she was curled into Chase's side. She had never been this attracted to a man and she felt like a teenage girl. She felt as though she was sixteen again and sitting next to the most beautiful boy in school. She felt jumpy, as if she had never been kissed or touched or made love to. She felt innocent, as though her heart had never been broken before.

She looked away from the television and up at his profile. His strong jaw, his clean-shaven face. Even though the only visible light in the room came from the television, she couldn't help notice how handsome he was. It was almost as if she was seeing him for the first time. And maybe she was. They had eaten one of the best dinners she had ever had. Crab-stuffed fried shrimp. Duck and andouille gumbo and smothered chicken with fresh hot rolls. For dessert they had shared coconut bread pudding. It was all delicious without being fussy. And there was Chase who made her laugh and was easy to talk to. He was relaxed, and he was fun to be with. She had misjudged him, thinking he was coldly handsome and unbearably stuffy. He had said something to her that had shaken her up. That she was the workaholic and he was the one who knew how to take time and enjoy things. She would never have thought of herself that way until he pointed it out.

He had a way of making her worldview shift with just a few words.

And the way he looked at her... She felt it all the way to her core.

You need someone to take care of you.

That comment should have made her angry. If anyone else had said it, it would have. But just for a moment she let herself imagine what it might be like if she let him take care of her, what it would be like if she came home to him every night and ate dinner with him and just talked about silly things with him.

They were more similar than they were different. It was funny how they'd ended up on such different paths that wound up crossing.

"You're looking at me," he said in the low voice of his that always warmed her insides.

She was busted. There was nothing she could do but admit to it. "I am. I like the way you look."

"I like the way you look, too." He looked at her, into her eyes, and wrapped one of her curls around his finger. "Don't look at me. It's very hard for me not to kiss you right now."

She wanted him to kiss her. The lights were dim.

There was no one around. They were pressed against each other like magnets. Nothing would be able to stop them once they got started. She didn't have enough will-power. Her body wanted to be loved.

But she knew she might get addicted. It had happened the last time. She had been so in love with Steven that she started to lose herself. She wore only what he liked and ate where he wanted and did what he wanted to do. His friends became her only friends.

She hadn't noticed when it happened, but little by little his control over her grew and she was living to make him happy. She'd never told anyone that. Not even her mother. She thought she was strong. She had tried to be strong, but she was afraid that with certain men she became weak, became blinded.

You won't make it in this world without me. You need me.

She kept hearing Steven's words. Seeing the disdain on his face whenever she did something that he was displeased with.

She was afraid that it could happen again with Chase. Not that he would mentally abuse her like that, but that she would allow herself to become so wrapped up in him that she would forget who she was.

And Amber didn't want to do that again. She had too much to accomplish to let that happen.

"Can I get you something to drink?" she asked him, needing to step away so she could clear her head. "Or would you like something to eat? I have popcorn. My mother made some of her world famous peach tea when she was here the other day. I can get you a glass of that."

He kissed her then. Ignoring her questions and what she wanted, but giving her what she needed. He cupped her face in his hands and swept his tongue deep inside her mouth. She moaned. She could feel herself melting. She couldn't help it. She reached for him, wrapping her arms around him, pulling him closer to her.

She didn't realize that he had shifted, that he was laying her down on the couch till she felt her back hit the cushion. She broke the kiss and looked up at him. Wanting to tell him to stop but unable to get the words out.

"No sex," he said. "I promise. But I've been looking at you all day and I know if I leave here tonight without touching you, I'll regret it and I don't want to be a man who lives his life with regrets."

She nodded and relaxed into the cushions. He felt good on top of her. Heavy. His body was hard and long and somehow fit hers perfectly. She wanted to wrap her legs around him, to feel him more, to feel him inside her, but he'd promised her no sex and she was going to trust him.

His lips brushed her throat and all coherent thoughts rushed from her head. He was a man who knew how to seduce, who knew how to get what he wanted—he had caused her to tip her chin upward, giving him more access to her throat as he slowly kissed every inch of it.

"Chase." She cried out his name as his hand reached beneath her tank top and grasped her breast, his thumb stroking her nipple through her bra, making it painfully hard. He was erect. She could feel him brushing between her legs, the heat of him. She rubbed against it, unable to stop herself. He broke the kiss and looked down at her, need in his eyes.

She wanted to take back what she'd said. She wanted to submit to the passion he built up inside her because in that moment she had forgotten all the reasons she should stay away.

He hands grabbed the hem of her skirt, hiking it up to reveal her underwear. "No sex. I promise you. I just want to touch you. Say you trust me."

She nodded, not caring if she trusted him or not. She wanted to feel his hands on her that badly.

"I need to hear you say it."

"I trust you."

"Good." He leaned down and gave her one long scorching kiss as he pulled off her underwear.

She was wet. She could smell the arousal in the air. Chase just knelt back and looked at her. She must have been a sight with her hair standing wildly all over her head, her skirt hiked up and her legs open to him. "Just so damn beautiful," he said as he exhaled.

He touched her between her legs, stroking the length of her, slipping his long thick finger inside of her. Her toes curled then. Her heart beat faster and she looked up at him, waiting impatiently for what he would do next.

He shifted his body again and she thought he was going to lower himself on top of her but he didn't. He settled his head between her legs, looking up at her once before he dipped his head and licked the place that throbbed for him.

She gasped, surprised that he did that and astounded at how amazing it felt. Steven had never done this to her, for her. He took and took and took and never gave. But Chase was giving to her and it was one hell of a present. He worked his tongue in connection with his fingers, bringing her right to the edge and backing her down. He was driving her insane and she could feel herself writhing against him and panting out his name. She forgot to be quiet. She forgot to temper her passion. She forgot to think.

He had that kind of effect on her.

"Please, Chase. Please." She wasn't sure what she was begging for. Release? For this to never end? Whatever it was, she couldn't help crying out his name.

Whatever it was, he seemed to know and he sucked her nub into his mouth, causing an orgasm to take over her body. The world slipped from beneath her then and she felt as if she was falling through air.

It took a while for her to come back down, but when she did, Chase was sitting over her, a tight look on his face. She knew what he needed. To be soothed. To have his own release. She reached for him, but he backed away. "You can't touch me. I made a promise to you and if you touch me, I'll break it. I'm a man of my word."

"It's okay." She held out her hand to him, but he walked away from her.

"I'm going to go now. I'll see you tomorrow." He walked out the door then.

But he still managed to surprise her because, when she walked outside the next day, he was waiting for her. He had come to take her to work.

Chapter 7

Chase could tell Amber was surprised to see him sitting on the steps of her porch the next morning. He had thought about her all night. He even saw her face in his dreams, and when he woke, his first thought was of her. But not those heated sexual thoughts that had kept him hard and wanting her all night. He remembered that she didn't have a car.

He was glad for the excuse to be here—now that he had tasted her, he knew he needed to have all of her.

"Good morning," she said with her eyes still wide. "You're here."

He stood up and looked at her. She wore a black shirt and a denim skirt that showed off her shapely legs and a pair of brightly colored flats. He felt his groin twitch. The memory of her lying on the couch, her skirt bunched up at her waist, entered his mind again. "You still don't have a car and I noticed that you are kind of far from public transportation."

"It's just a few blocks or so."

"Eleven."

"Good exercise. I need to work off all that dinner we ate yesterday. Thank you, by the way. I don't know if I told you that. For the ride. For dinner. For…dessert."

He grinned at her. "Are we going to talk about that? About…dessert?"

"There's nothing to talk about. It was just one friend doing a very nice favor for another."

"Oh. Is that what we're going to call it?"

She nodded. "That's what we're going to call it."

"Okay then." He stepped forward, slid his hand into her thick curls and kissed her. She placed her hand over his, shut her eyes and let herself be kissed. He was glad they were standing outside on her porch. He was glad that she had to be to work in a few minutes because, if she hadn't, he would have tumbled her into bed and not let her out until dinnertime.

"Chase," she groaned with her eyes half closed.

"I'm sorry, Amber, but I'm going to kiss you like that every day until you tell me it's okay to do more."

She looked into his eyes for a moment and he knew that there must be a million thoughts going through her head, but he couldn't tell what she was thinking. She just nodded and said, "Let's go to work."

They arrived at work a few minutes later and for a moment he was tempted to linger behind and let her walk in alone, but he didn't care who saw them walk in together. Not even Mariah, who was behind the counter placing a fresh tray of Draynuts, her invention of croissant-doughnuts, beneath the glass. "Well, good morning, you two."

Chase couldn't help but note the curious look in his sister's eyes and, unlike with Amber, he knew exactly what she was thinking.

What the hell are you doing with my friend?

"Hey, girl," Amber said as she clocked in behind the counter. "You know my car broke down again. I came back here yesterday to ask you for a ride, but you had already left. I had to ask Chase to take me to the community center."

Amber was smart, cutting his sister off at the pass so that she didn't have anything to say. He liked that.

"Oh, I'm sorry. I cannot believe your car broke down again! You should really think about getting a new one. I don't want to hear someday that you got stranded alone in the middle of the night."

"I love my little bug and I can't afford a new car. I'm not even sure I can afford the repairs on this one."

"What can't you afford?" Jackson walked in from the back, wearing expensive jeans and a T-shirt that seemed to be his uniform lately. He wrapped his arm around Amber in a way that would seem intimate to anybody. Chase knew that was just how Jackson was, and yet seeing his brother with his arm wrapped around her made him want to knock him on his head.

"A new car. Mine broke down again. Your brother was nice enough to give me a ride."

"I thought I saw you leaving here last night with

Chase. I thought it was for a good reason, but I should have known it wasn't with my brother."

"What's that supposed to mean?" Amber asked, seeming curious.

"You're fine, Amber. If Chase was smart he would have taken you out. He would have wined and dined you, but if my brother is too stupid to do it, I will. Let me take you out. I'll show you a good time."

Chase reached over and smacked Jackson in the back of the head. "Watch yourself, little brother. Just because I'm good at math doesn't mean I can't kick your behind."

"You hit me." Jackson looked truly surprised. "Mariah, he hit me."

"He did hit you. Stop being fresh with Amber. There are a million women in Seattle you can dip your fishing pole into. Why can't you look outside the bakery?"

Chase knew Mariah had said that for his benefit, too, but he was the oldest, and he didn't have to listen to her. "I'm going to conference in with the managers of the Chicago and LA branches of Lillian's so we can get our heads around our next marketing strategy. I wanted to see what worked for them and what didn't, so we can plan our next move. I would like both of you there when I speak to them."

"I'll be there," Mariah said. "Jackson and I have been conferring on some new recipes. He wants to expand the menu and offer different specialty items each month. I'm leaning toward doing a few things well to ensure quality."

"Both are valid points. Amber, what do you think?"

"Me?" She pointed to herself.

"Yes, you. You manage our coffee café. We would like your input."

"I think they are both great ideas. What about rolling out one specialty bakery item a month in conjunction with a specialty coffee drink? We could do some seasonal things that aren't done at the other Myers stores."

"We could call it dessert pairings or something to that effect," Jackson said. "Like wine pairings but sweet. What kind of flavors were you thinking of?"

"Summer is coming. I was thinking of doing some frozen drinks and really playing with our iced coffee flavors. Like ice-cream-flavored coffees. I think I could be successful in making a cookies-and-cream flavored iced coffee."

"I like that." Jackson nodded. "I have been thinking of doing a cookies-and-cream brownie with a ganache icing. What do you think, Mariah?"

"I like the idea, too. We can also do a more chocolaty version. With fudge and a cookie right in the middle as sort of a filling."

Chase watched as the ideas sprung from his siblings. They talked about catchy names and flavors, their creativity blooming before him. He envied them. He didn't have that, but he had the focus to pull all the ideas together. "Amber, can you make a list of seasonal drinks and flavors and get that to me before the end of the week?"

"I can."

"Jackson, Mariah, I would like you each to come up with twelve promotional products we can sell. They don't have to be crazy creative but something we can do at not a lot of cost that we can upsell."

"It won't be a problem. Jackson has so many ideas it might be hard for us to narrow it down. You should hear some of the stuff he's coming up with for his cupcake bite for Bite of Seattle."

"Sweet potato cupcake with a marshmallow frosting," Jackson said proudly. "Like having Thanksgiving anytime."

"That actually sounds amazing, Jackson," Amber said. "I would love to try one."

"Me, too. I need Mariah's help nailing down some of the flavors."

"Your palate is better than mine, Jack. You just have to spend some time in the kitchen." She looked at Chase. "How's your cupcake idea coming?"

It wasn't. His mind was completely blank when it came to an idea for his mini cupcake. "I'm thinking about it."

"Okay." Mariah didn't look convinced. "Let me know and we can start playing around in the test kitchen."

He nodded. "I have to start working."

"Wait. I wanted us all to go out to dinner in a couple of days. We got a babysitter for EJ. Is everyone still free this week?"

Chase tried not to look at Amber, but he couldn't help it. He would take her out to dinner every night this week if she would let him. She was protecting herself, keeping herself away from him even though the pull between them was so strong. If it were any other woman he would think that she was playing games. He wasn't into games. He didn't have time for them. But he knew that wasn't what Amber was doing. He was going to have to work hard for her.

He welcomed the challenge, because he knew that the best things in life were the ones you worked the hardest for.

"Excuse me? How much is it going to cost?" Amber asked her mechanic for the second time. She wasn't sure she had heard him correctly.

He repeated the price and she knew her hearing was fine, but her stomach had certainly taken a turn for the worse.

"Can you just give me a report of what needs to be fixed? I'm going to have it towed home."

Thirty-six hundred dollars. She didn't have thirty-six hundred dollars. She would never have that much money. She was doomed to take the bus forever.

She walked in through the back door of the bakery, her head running through the numbers, wondering if she had anything of value that she could sell for quick cash. But there was nothing. Nothing but the jewelry she made and that wasn't quick cash. It would be another couple of weeks before she would get any money from the boutiques that were carrying her pieces.

"Hey." She smashed into a hard chest and then felt strong hands grip her shoulders, steadying her. "Are you okay?"

She looked up to see Chase standing there, although she had known that it was Chase before her eyes had focused on his face. She had come to know his scent and for some reason she found it soothing. "I'm fine."

"You're not." He shook his head, his eyes filled with more concern than she would like. "What's wrong?"

"I…" She thought about brushing him off, but she couldn't bring herself to. "I just got off the phone with my mechanic. It's going to cost all my arms and legs to get it fixed."

"What's wrong with it?"

"I think the list of what's right with it is shorter. It needs new guts. I'm not sure what I'm going to do."

She didn't realize that she had rested her head on his chest until she felt his lips brush her forehead. "What can I do?"

"Nothing." She wrapped her arms around him. "This is enough."

She shut her eyes, allowing herself to completely relax into him. She couldn't think of the last time she had leaned on anyone, the last time she felt comfortable enough to lean on anyone. "Is it wrong for me to be secretly glad that your car is not working? I've never looked forward to carpooling so much."

She felt herself smiling. When he had dropped her off last night, that was it. She hadn't invited him up. She hadn't lingered any longer than she should have, and yet it didn't stop the constant thoughts of him. It didn't stop her from wishing that she wasn't lying alone in her bed. It didn't stop her from feeling unsatisfied when she woke up this morning. And it certainly didn't stop her heart from lifting when she'd seen him waiting on her steps when she walked out of her building.

"Oh, excuse me," she heard Mariah say. "Am I interrupting something?"

"No. I'm hugging your brother in the hallway in the back of your very busy bakery because I'm having a crappy day."

"You could talk to me about your bad day."

"I don't want to talk. I just wanted to hug your brother." She lifted her head to look at her friend. "We're not sleeping together, Mariah. But if we ever do get to that point, I want you to be okay with it. And I want you to think that Chase and I would go into it with our eyes open and that we are both levelheaded enough to handle whatever comes our way."

Mariah looked taken aback for a moment, but she nodded. "Of course. I trust you both. Can't blame a girl for being curious, can you?"

"I blame your birth for most of the things that have gone wrong in my life," Chase said with a smile as his sister's eyes widened.

"You're joking, aren't you?"

"I am."

"Oh." Mariah grinned at him. "If you've got a few minutes, Jackson wants us to try the cupcake recipes he's been toying with."

"You come, too, Amber."

"Okay. I will."

"We'll be there in a moment," Chase said, looking down at Amber. After Mariah's heels clicked away, he spoke again. "I'm feeling the need to kiss you right now." And then he did and then she got swept away for a moment, even though it was a soft, simple kiss.

He had that effect on her. He made her forget herself. He made her forget everything and that wasn't good for her.

She broke the kiss. "I didn't say I was going to sleep with you, you know," she said, trying to keep her voice light.

"I know, and I'm hoping you know that I don't just want sex from you."

He could get that from any woman. But he seemed to like her and she couldn't figure out why. In the back of her head, she knew that the tiny bit of self-doubt was left over from Steven. He had tried to make her feel as if she was nothing without him. As though she couldn't survive on her own. He had stripped little pieces of her away without her even noticing, and that scared her.

She'd thought she was stronger than that. And that's why she was so afraid of Chase. He really was the type of man she could lose her heart to. It wasn't easy to stay away from him when her body ached to be near his. It would be hard to keep him at arm's length when all she wanted to be was close.

She could get firm. She could put her foot down, tell him that it was never going to happen, but she had started this. She had slid the coffee in front of him that night. She had come to him when her car broke down. She had invited him into her home that night. She had wrapped her arms around him.

"I would love to know what's going on in that head of yours."

"It's a complicated mess."

"Well, maybe I'm in the mood for complications."

She swallowed hard. Chase Drayson was not going to leave her without taking a piece of her heart.

Chapter 8

"This place," Amber said as she looked around Chase's condo the next evening, "It makes my apartment look like a dingy little shoe box."

Chase watched her wide eyes as she took it all in. He kind of felt a rush at seeing her in his space. With a small duffel bag in her hands. He wished she held it because she was planning to stay the night, but she had it for a much more innocent reason. They were all going out to dinner tonight and instead of her changing her clothes in the bakery bathroom he had invited her to do so here. He had to change anyway. He had read up on the restaurant that Jackson had picked for them, and he knew that it was a place where people dressed to impress.

"I like your place. It feels lived in," he said.

She nodded and turned around to smile at him. "I agree. Those dirty dishes in the sink give it a real homey feel."

He grinned back at her. He found smiling easier with her. "Can I offer you something to drink? I've got a fully stocked bar."

"You just want to get me tipsy so I'll let you have your way with me," she teased with a smile curling her lips.

"No." He shook his head. "If you ever give me the chance to be with you, I want you stone-cold sober so your mind can be clear and remember every touch and kiss I give you."

She looked at him for a long moment and he could see the need in her eyes, or maybe that was his own lust mirrored in them. There had been a slight tension in the air since they entered his home. Like there was every time they were completely alone. In private where no one could hear what they said or see what they did. If he wanted to, he could just pick her up and carry her to his bedroom, or lay her down on his couch and strip off the flowy skirt she had on, or take her into his steam shower and make love to her up against the wall.

"Water," she said, snapping him out of his thoughts.

"What?"

They weren't anywhere near touching and yet she took a step backward. "D-do you have any water? My mouth has gone dry."

She had the opposite effect on him. His watered whenever he was around her. "Still or sparkling?"

"Sparkling, please."

"Sit down, Amber. I'm not going to bite you."

"I might like it if you did and that's what I'm afraid of."

He wanted to ask her what her plan was for them, but he knew better than to push her. He had to give Amber time. Normally he would have moved on by now, but he wouldn't with her, because he felt as though she would be worth the wait. "Lemon?" he asked as he walked to the bar, trying push away the image of him playfully sinking his teeth into her behind.

"You might spoil me," she said as he handed her a glass of premium sparkling water with a wedge of lemon placed on the rim of the glass. "I feel quite classy when I'm with you, Chase."

"Do you? As opposed to any other time?"

"I forget that I'm just a barista and my jewelry business is at a standstill. I forget that I'm a grad student with loans I might never be able to pay off and a car that doesn't work. You treat me as an equal."

"Why wouldn't I?"

"It's just that my ex…" She trailed off with a shake of her head. "Never mind."

"What? Tell me."

"You don't want to hear about my ex."

"I do. I wouldn't have asked you if I didn't."

She hesitated for a moment. "He just thought I wasn't on his level."

"I just can't see you with anyone like that." A thought occurred to him. "Is that why you're hesitant about us? Do you think I'm pretentious?"

"No, Chase." She set her glass down on the bar and

leaned across to kiss his cheek. "You're kind and generous and I wouldn't allow you to schlep me back and forth to work if I thought you were."

He resisted the urge to cup her face in his hands and pull her into a long kiss, but they had to be at the restaurant in an hour and he knew better than to start something that he couldn't take his sweet time to finish. "I'm going to go get ready now. There's a bathroom in the second bedroom you can use, or a smaller one in the hallway. There are fresh washcloths and towels in each bathroom as well as soap and toothbrushes."

"Wow," she said with a small smile. "Better than a hotel. Thank you, Chase."

"What are you thanking me for? I haven't done anything."

"No? Maybe I just feel like thanking you for being my friend." He nodded and walked away from her to get ready. If he hadn't, there was no way they were making it to dinner on time.

Chase emerged a half hour later freshly showered and ready to spend the evening with his siblings. Amber was sitting on the edge of his couch, looking far sexier than when he'd left her.

"Hey." She stood when she saw him and a pure surge of need filled him as he studied her. The first thing he noticed was her hair. Her curls were wilder tonight, much different from the way she wore her hair at the bakery, and she had on the slightest bit of makeup that enhanced her natural beauty. On her body was a short black silky shirt dress that was printed with a vibrant pattern in a few strategic places. It wasn't tight. It didn't cling to her body, rather it skimmed, keeping with her bohemian style and bringing out her sex appeal in a subtle way.

"Hey. You look great."

"Thank you. You do, too," she said shyly. "I wasn't sure what to wear. I thought maybe this wasn't right."

He reached for her hand, liking the way it felt tucked into his. "It's right. It's perfect. Let's go."

The restaurant was in one of downtown Seattle's trendiest neighborhoods, filled with good-looking young people ready to enjoy a night out. This was a section of town Chase rarely ventured into anymore, preferring quieter small restaurants with a reputation for great food, but Jackson was always in search of the trendiest new spot. He wouldn't be surprised if his brother had been an early investor in this place. Chase might have the head for business and numbers, but Jackson was the one who had a knack for seeing the potential in something. That's why he had done so well with his investments. He took risky gambles that paid off and then got out quickly before he was hit. It probably had a little something to do with his past as a high-stakes poker player.

"Do you know this place?" Amber asked as they walked in.

"No. I know nothing about it. I'm not the foodie in the family. If Jackson is onto this place, it's probably about to blow up and we won't be able to get in again without being put on a waitlist."

She nodded. "It looks amazing." She was right; the decor was done in a way that transported the diners to eastern Asia. It was exotic, with antique wall hangings and small screens and pagodas. They were escorted downstairs to a quieter dining room. Chase wasn't one for design details, but even he noticed the white leather and wooden chairs that looked to be custom-made for the restaurant. "This is the perfect place to take an ugly date," Amber joked in Chase's ear. "The mood lighting makes it hard to see what you're really working with."

Chase laughed, but he also grew a little aroused. She smelled good, like soap and clean skin and a little something sensual. Her breast had pressed into his arm as she spoke and her warm sweet breath on his ear almost made it hard for him to concentrate on what she was saying, but he knew he had to keep all those feelings in check tonight.

Mariah and her fiancé would be there tonight, probably watching everything they did and speculating on what was going on. Not that Chase cared or felt that he had to go out of his way to explain things to his sister, but for Amber's sake he would go through the evening as if they were just friends and nothing more.

When she was ready he wouldn't hold back. He would let the world know that she was his and he was hers. He kept thinking back to what she had almost said about her ex. He wanted to press her on it. There was more to her story, more than that he just wasn't supportive. Although that was enough to cause a breakup, but Chase had a feeling that this guy had really hurt her.

"Hi, you two!" Mariah stood up when she spotted them. His sister was looking beautiful and classic in a blush-colored cocktail dress. "Isn't this place something?"

"It is." Amber quickly hugged Everett and Mariah. "I wonder how long it took to design it."

"Three years," Jackson said from behind them. "The owners consulted with the famed Argentinean designer Jacques Perez. Half of the battle was finding the right space, in the right part of Seattle, that could encompass his vision."

"And how do you know so much about this, Jackson?" Amber asked.

"I know a little bit about everything," he responded with a wink. "And might I add that you are looking especially fine tonight, Miss Amber. I know my brother is proud to be walking in tonight with a woman like you on his arm."

"Tell me, did you take lessons to become so charming, or does this stuff just come out of you naturally?"

A wide grin spread across Jackson's face. "Do I look like the type of man who took any sort of lessons? I did my time in school and got out. Sit." He motioned to a chair. "I've got some special drinks coming."

"Speaking of school," Everett said, "how is the MBA coming?"

"I'm almost done with this semester. I've got one final left and a paper due next week."

"I don't know how you do it," Chase said. "I remember my MBA program. It was tough and I didn't have to worry about a full-time job, teaching a class and running my own business."

"I get by with a little help from my friends. You all have been great with accommodating my schedule."

"When we see potential in someone, we all do what has to be done," Everett said.

A waiter came then with a pitcher of passion fruit sangria and glasses of lychee-raspberry Bellinis. "I'll be back to take your orders momentarily."

It was then they picked up their menus, which listed delicacies from all over Asia.

"There's some à la carte stuff, but I thought we all could try the chef's choice tasting menu," Jackson said as Chase's eyes went to that section.

It was a ten-course menu filled with summer lobster rolls and pork belly steamed buns and sashimi.

He heard Amber make a soft noise of distress, and when he looked up at her, he knew there was something wrong.

He placed his hand on her knee. The others hadn't noticed because they were talking about the menu choices. "What is it?"

She leaned over, speaking into his ear. "This says eighty-five dollars a person."

"Yes." He hadn't looked at the price, but he knew that restaurants that looked like this charged prices like that.

"I can't afford that. I have to work hours and hours to make that kind of money."

"Don't worry about it. I'm paying."

"I don't want you to pay for me. It makes me uncomfortable."

"I'll pay for everyone."

He looked into her face, surprised that she looked so upset about it. He was blessed with money. He worked hard and invested wisely. He could afford dinners like this. He could afford to spoil her and, more important, he wanted to. He wanted to fix her car and for her not to worry about her student loan debt. He wanted her to be comfortable.

"What?"

"That makes me feel even worse."

"I have it and Jackson has it and Everett has it to spend. Mariah has invested smartly, too. We've done well for ourselves."

"And it makes me feel like I don't belong here."

He had never expected her to say that. "Why? You work for everything you have just like we do. There's no difference."

"Our bank accounts beg to differ."

"What are you two whispering about over there?" Mariah asked, looking suspicious.

"I wasn't feeling well before we left," Chase answered. "Amber was just checking up on me."

"What's the matter, Chase?" The look in his sister's eyes changed to one of concern.

"It's my head, but now that I'm sitting here and smelling all this food, my stomach is not feeling too great, either."

"Spicy Asian food probably isn't the best for it," Everett said.

"I didn't want to cancel because I was looking forward to this evening." He looked back to Amber. "I think it's only going to get worse. Would you mind driving me home?"

She didn't say anything, she just nodded and placed her hand on his cheek.

"You're never sick, Chase," Mariah said, looking concerned. "I hope it's not serious."

"I think it's just a bug," he said, standing. "We had better go." He took his keys out of his pocket, handing them to Amber.

He had looked forward to eating here with his siblings tonight, but making Amber happy had trumped that.

Chapter 9

Amber slipped her hand into Chase's as soon as they were out of his siblings' line of sight. He didn't say anything, just stroked his thumb along hers. She didn't know what was going through his head, but she knew what was going through hers, and it was guilt. She hadn't meant for him to leave his family just because she was uncomfortable with the high price tag of dinner. She should have just shut up and let him pay. She knew the Draysons had all worked for their money, but they had also come from money, while she had come from working-class people. People who had to work all day just to make what the Draysons were going to spend on dinner for one person.

"You didn't have to do that," she said once they left the restaurant.

"I did." She was half waiting for him to show anger or annoyance with her. If he were Steven, he would accuse her of not having enough class to be there, but then again, if he were Steven, he would never have left the restaurant at all, no matter what she was feeling.

"I feel foolish now. I didn't mean to ruin your night. You can take me right home and I'll take the bus tomorrow morning."

He stopped walking and looked down into her eyes. "Why are you punishing me?"

She blinked at him. "Punishing you?"

"You don't want me taking you to work anymore. That's punishing me."

"I feel like I'm inconveniencing you!"

"You're not inconveniencing me. You think I would be going out of my way to give you a ride if there wasn't something in it for me? Plus, eighty-five dollars is a lot to spend on one meal for one person, and I'm glad we left because I can get three times as much food for half the price at the local spot around the corner from my condo."

"Oh, can you?"

"Yeah, and if you think you're getting out of my buying you dinner tonight, you're dead wrong."

"Chase…" Each sweet thing that he said made her feel a little worse. "It's okay to be annoyed with me."

"I'm not annoyed with you. I just want to know why you can't let me buy you dinner."

"Because we are at such different points in our lives. You sign my paychecks. You have everything and I have nothing and I want to feel like your equal, and tonight in there I didn't. There was so much success around me and I felt like I was the barista charity case who couldn't afford to be there."

"If you don't feel like you belong, then I feel like I don't belong. But I do feel like I belong with you. I don't care where we spend the evening as long as I get to spend it with you."

Her heart flipped over in her chest and she knew she was in trouble because she felt herself slipping a tiny bit into love with him. She leaned in and kissed his lips softly. "I would very much like to buy your dinner tonight, Mr. Drayson."

"Only if you let me buy yours tomorrow, Ms. Bernard."

"I think I can do that."

Chase took her back to his place and handed her the menu to his favorite Chinese restaurant before he left the room without a word. She used his fancy house phone to make the call, ordering way too much food, but feeling that she needed to make up for the ten fancy courses that he was missing out on tonight because of her.

She took another look around his apartment now that he wasn't there to study her as she did. It was gorgeous, luxurious to say the least. It looked like a place a very rich man would stay. It looked like a place a working artist would never rest her head and yet she was here tonight, looking at the beautiful expensive art he had hanging on his walls and the sofa made of Italian leather and the carpet that was so plush and soft she knew she could curl up and fall asleep on it.

She walked behind the bar where she had seen him earlier and ran her hands along the colorful bottles. She recognized the names of some as top-shelf, others were in foreign languages that she didn't understand, but she was sure that they were high quality and probably tasted as beautiful as their packages looked.

"Did you want something to drink? Please help yourself."

She turned to look at him to see that he had changed. Her mouth went dry. He was in a sleeveless gray undershirt and gray checked sleep pants, his muscular arms and hard chest on display.

He had the body of an athlete and that surprised her. She knew he was in good shape, but seeing him now, out of all his buttoned-up attire, made heat curl in her belly and her body want to rub up against his. He was holding something in his hand but she barely noticed because she was so preoccupied by his spectacular form.

"What's that?" she asked him, trying to hide the desire that crept into her voice.

He stepped behind the bar into her space, so close to her that the warmth of his body heated hers. "I want you to put this on. I would like you to stay this evening. I'm not asking you to sleep with me, but I'm asking you to sleep here, to eat dinner with me and sit on the couch and watch stupid TV and just be here tonight."

"Your guest room is pretty nice." She took the T-shirt from him and looped her arms around his neck.

"My guest room *is* pretty nice," he said, kissing her throat. The closeness with him was erotic. Her nipples grew hard as she pressed her breasts against him.

Her thin dress suddenly seemed too hot, like too much clothing for her, and she wanted strip down for some relief but she knew that if her nude body got anywhere close to his, she would not cool down. She would only get hotter.

"Let me go change." She stepped away from him, not because she wanted to, but because being that close to him scrambled her senses.

She slipped into the hall bathroom and took off her dress, knowing that being here with him tonight, even if they didn't sleep together, was crossing a line that they could never uncross. Hell, they had probably already crossed that point the night she let him strip off her underwear and give her an orgasm she wouldn't soon forget. But tonight she was going to turn her brain off. Not think about anything at all, save enjoying this night with him.

When she emerged from the bathroom, she found Chase setting food out on his coffee table and sticking forks into the open cartons. There were no plates and she realized that tonight all formality had gone out the window. She didn't work for him. His sister wasn't her best friend and their lives weren't vastly different. Tonight they were just a man and a woman sharing a meal.

He looked up from his task, his eyes drinking her in. She couldn't help but notice that his eyes lingered on her bare legs. Her dress had been shorter than Chase's long T-shirt, but she could see the desire in his eyes. She could feel her own rising, knowing that there was nothing between her skin and his soft shirt.

"You ordered my favorites," he said after a long moment.

"I ordered everything. I don't want you missing out on your ten courses."

"I'm not missing out. In fact I think I'm gaining something extra."

"Indigestion?"

He laughed. He had a great deep laugh that sort of rumbled in his chest. She felt it go through her body and it warmed her. It was the type of laugh that she could listen to forever.

"Sit. I'll grab some wine. Red or white?"

"What kind goes the best with greasy takeout?"

"Beer."

She grinned at him. "Then beer it is."

He grabbed two bottles from the small fridge behind his bar, popped the tops off and took a seat beside her on the couch. He didn't give her any space, sitting as close to her as he could get. Her naked thigh pressed against his hard, clothed leg and suddenly she found it very hard to think straight. She could only feel. Feel her heart beating faster. Feel her nipples turn into rock-hard peaks, feel that gentle throb between her legs.

She was hungry, but it wasn't for the feast spread out in front of them on Chase's coffee table.

"I have a friend who brews his own stuff. He wants to open a gastropub in the near future and sell this beer. I'm thinking about investing."

"Oh. Are you?" She took of sip of her beer. It had a slightly sweet citrusy flavor. It was enjoyable, but right now she wasn't all that thirsty.

"I am…" He trailed off as she stood up and removed his T-shirt from her body. It had been a very long time since she had stood before a man naked. The last time she had she'd felt self-conscious, wondering if her ex was going to criticize, but she felt none of that standing before Chase. She felt confident. She felt sexy.

"When a woman gets naked in front of a man, she expects him to say something."

"Thank you," he said slowly.

She laughed as he grabbed her hand and tugged her into his lap. She felt his erection rubbing against her bottom. She couldn't help but move against it. His breath quickened and he let out a tiny moan that excited her even more.

"Are you sure about this?" He placed his hand on her thigh, stroking it with his thumb.

"I think we both knew this was happening tonight." She ran her hand over his hard pecs. "You're a beautiful man, Chase." She kissed his throat, his powerful Adam's apple that she had dreamed about kissing since the first time they had had a conversation. "Not just on the outside, but you are kind and thoughtful and sweet, and I would like nothing more than to be with you tonight."

He said nothing to that, just got up with her in his arms and carried her to his bedroom. His room screamed masculinity, done in all grays and blacks, but she had a hard time taking it all in because he had dropped her on the bed and covered her body with his own.

She moaned at the feel of his weight on top of her. He was heavy, but the most wonderful kind of heavy that made her feel protected and grounded.

He took her mouth in a hard, hot kiss, robbing her of her breath and her senses. She melted into the mattress, letting him take what he wanted from her. She could taste his need, his hunger for her. She wanted to satisfy him. She wanted to fulfill his every desire tonight.

"Wrap your legs around me," he panted when he broke the kiss. "I want to feel more of you."

She did as he asked and he slid his hands to her behind, cupping it, squeezing her flesh as he stroked his hardness between her legs. The fact that he was fully clothed while she was naked making it hotter. But still she wanted to feel his skin, feel his entire body pressed against hers with no barriers between them.

"Take this off." She tugged at his shirt. He let her pull it off him, but he didn't return to his spot on top of her. He knelt between her legs and stroked one of his big hands up her rib cage.

"There's so much I want to kiss and touch. I'm not sure where to begin."

"Let me help you decide." She got up on her knees so that she faced him, and kissed him softly just before she took hold of his fingers and ran them across her nipples. "Here is good. I like the way that feels."

"What about this?" He cupped her breast and lowered his head, taking her tight little point into his mouth and sucking gently. She trembled. His warm wet mouth, his smooth tongue, the way his eyes closed when he tasted her all brought her that much closer to climax, and he had barely touched her yet.

"Chase," she whimpered as she pulled away from him and grasped his face to pull him in for another kiss.

The only way she could describe the way he kissed her was erotic. It was slow and fast at the same time. His tongue thrust in and out of her mouth, his hands stroked her body. The experience made her think that every other kiss she'd had and every other kiss she might have would never compare to his.

"I need you, Amber." She slipped her hand inside his pants, finding his hard cock and stroking it. She loved the way it twitched in her hand. She loved the deep moan that escaped him.

"Enough." He stopped her. "I'm too far gone. I need this to last."

"I don't." She placed his hand between her thighs so he could feel how wet she was. "I'm ready."

"Amber." She stroked herself with his fingers, pleasuring herself while she was taking pleasure in watching him watch her.

"I imagined this, Chase." She slid his finger inside of her. "I imagined you here. Even when I didn't want to. Even though you're the last thing I should be thinking about." She pumped his fingers a little faster as she felt her orgasm growing closer.

He let out an almost primal grunt, pushed her backward on the bed and then ripped open his nightstand to pull out a condom. She had never seen this side of him. Buttoned-up Chase Drayson was hot and hard and uninhibited and it was so sexy it was almost scary. He put the condom on and covered her body, sliding into her so hard she saw stars. But it was a good kind of hard. His slid out slowly so that she felt every single inch and slammed into her once again.

She cried out. She dug her nails in his back. She writhed beneath him. She didn't want it to end. But Chase was too good. His strokes too efficient. She was trying to prolong it, tried to make it last longer, but he kept driving into her with that toe-curling pace.

He looked down into her eyes, his face twisted with pleasure. He was so beautiful and she was so close to release. He was inside of her. He was as close to her as two people could get and yet she wanted more. To be completely with him as orgasm struck. She couldn't help but pull his head down to hers and kiss his lips.

It was a wild kiss, as though he was giving her his all. She didn't hold back, either. She wouldn't allow herself to hold back.

Her climax struck her with a force that took her breath away. He came with her, crying out her name as he did.

He collapsed on top of her, his body going boneless. She loved the feeling of him on her, still inside of her, his breath brushing her skin.

After a while he rolled off her, and she mourned the loss of his skin pressed against hers. But apparently he hadn't liked the space between them, either, because he gathered her close and buried his face in her neck, leaving behind sweet tiny kisses. "You know this isn't going to be just one night, right? I don't think I'm going to be able to get enough of you."

She didn't think she was going to be able to get enough of him, either, and that scared her.

Chapter 10

For the first time in his adult life, Chase had called out of work when he wasn't sick. But he had a good reason and she had her buttery soft legs spread across his lap. Amber had spent the night in his bed wrapped in his arms. They had made love four times that night, and when they woke up this morning, he knew he couldn't let her leave. He wanted nothing more than to just spend the entire day alone with her. No interruptions. None of the stressors of the outside world infiltrating.

"What do you think about peppermint peach?" Chase asked her as his pencil moved across his notepad."

"For a cupcake? It's very interesting." Amber looked up at him with her brows raised. He could tell she thought it was a bad idea, but she didn't want to hurt his feelings. "I'm glad you're really thinking about this."

"You can tell me it's bad."

"How would I know if it's bad or not? I haven't tasted it. It could be the best cupcake on earth."

She was sweet and he found himself completely re-laxed for once. That was a rarity for him. It must have been her. No one else could put him at such ease.

"I'm taking this seriously. I even made a sketch." He turned his pad around for her to see the drawing he'd made of the cupcake. Amber carried around colored pencils in that huge bag she always had with her just in case the idea for a design popped into her mind. He thought she was crazy when she suggested they spend the afternoon coloring, but forty minutes into it he had to admit he was having fun.

"That's beautiful. I love the way you have the candy cane sticking in the icing. Maybe we can try to make them this evening."

"I think it will be gross, but if we launch a success-ful marketing campaign we could get everyone talk-ing about it. Lillian's: Home of the Peachy Peppermint Pastry."

"I find it sexy the way you use alliteration, baby." She leaned closer to him and kissed the crease of his neck. It turned him on. Everything she did turned him on. He couldn't get enough of her and they spent the day together, eating leftover Chinese food and making love all over his apartment. He kept his cellphone on silent. His email had gone unchecked and unanswered for the first time in his adult life and he just laid around with someone.

He never allowed himself to do this. His mind had

always wandered to what he was going to do next, what had to be done, how he could have perfected the things he'd already accomplished. But not today. Today none of that mattered.

"This Bite of Seattle is really important to you, isn't it? You've thought of a hundred cupcake ideas in the past half hour."

"It's not just important to me, it's important for Lillian's. We try not to talk about it there, but Sweetness Bakery is our direct competition and I've been hearing that some of our recipes are extremely close to theirs. But having frequented their business before we opened ours, I know they didn't have those items on their menus until recently."

"Like what?"

"I overheard a customer asking one of our cashiers about the strawberry lemon cake truffles. They wanted to know if we had gotten the idea from Sweetness, but I was there when Mariah and Jackson thought up the idea. I know Sweetness didn't offer that before. We checked out all the area bakery menus and that was our original idea."

"Hmm. Do you think there is a spy or something? Maybe one of Sweetness's people came in and ordered it and then tried to replicate it."

"Maybe." He nodded. "But it's kind of a blatant rip-off, isn't it? I think it could be an inside job."

"Really?"

"We hired a new girl a few weeks back. She seems innocent, but you never know." He shook his head. "I'm

probably just being paranoid. I don't really think anyone is trying to steal our recipes."

"Caring about the bakery is your job and I love that
you take so much pride in it." She cupped his face in
her hands and kissed his lips. "But we're not thinking
about anything today. No work. No worries. It's just
you and me and some Chinese food."

"You're right." He pulled her down on top of him,
and spread himself out on the couch. All that softness
against him caused him to let out a small groan. She
felt so good it was almost painful. "Kiss me again."

"As you wish, sir." She kissed him a little longer this
time, her tongue slipping into his mouth in a slow, erotic
way that made him hard all over again.

"Where did you learn how to kiss like that?" He slid
his hands under the T-shirt she was wearing and cupped
her perfectly round behind.

"Art school." She lifted her head and smiled down
at him. "It's a mandatory freshman class."

"Where did you go to school?"

"The Pratt Institute."

"Oh," he said, impressed. "You are as brilliant as
you are beautiful."

"Stop being so nice to me, Chase." She kissed his
lips lightly. "I don't know how to handle it."

"I don't want to stop. It's going to be impossible
for me."

"You're going to have to. I can't handle it."

"Why not?" He tried to keep the suspicion out of
his voice.

"Because it's going to make me need to have sex

with you right now. Not want, but need. And the pizza guy will be here any moment."

"You can stay here until he does." He slid his hands farther up her naked back, stroking her smooth skin.

"You're insatiable," she moaned.

"Am I too much?"

"You're just right." His heart pounded faster as she dipped her tongue into his mouth and kissed him again. He wasn't sure what it was about her, but there was definitely something about her that made him think that they could be in this for the long haul.

There was a knock at his door and he sighed, knowing that they were going to have to postpone their lovemaking for a few minutes.

"I'll get it." She grabbed her wallet out of her bag and hurried to the door. She was wearing just his T-shirt. Her hair was wild and he knew she wore nothing beneath. But she wasn't self-conscious about answering the door like that and he found it sexy as hell.

"Well, look what we have here," Jackson said, walking through the door, followed by Mariah. "You must have made one hell of a recovery, big brother. Or did Amber nurse you back to health?" He looked Amber up and down once. "And might I mention how gorgeous you are looking this afternoon, Amber?"

Mariah said nothing, but he could see the judgment in her eyes.

"What are you two doing here unannounced?"

"It's not unannounced." Mariah finally spoke. "We've been calling you all day. You haven't answered once. We were worried about you."

"Oh. My phones are on silent."

"And now we know why. Hey, girl," she said to Amber.

"We're adults," Amber said as she went to stand by Chase. "We like each other. Just be happy for us."

Mariah nodded. "I love you both."

There was another knock at the door and this time Chase went to answer it. "Good. Now join us for dinner. We ordered way too much from the pizza place."

Amber walked down her street after getting off the bus a few evenings later. She had just come from her last class of the semester where she had handed in her final paper and taken the most difficult final of her life. She thought she'd done okay. Not spectacular but pretty well. Chase had helped her study. She didn't think he would be a good study partner because he looked at her too long and she tumbled into bed with him. But when it was time to get down to business, Chase did not play. He was a surprisingly good teacher. Sometimes people who were extremely smart weren't good teachers because they thought everyone's mind should work the way theirs did. But Chase broke things down so that she understood them. He gave her little tricks to remember terms. He was a great teacher. She wanted to approach him about maybe taking on a mentee at the afterschool center or teaching a class about running a small business. But she knew that was asking him too much.

He had been a prince this past week. He picked her up and dropped her off at work, the community center and school. He had taken her grocery shopping and even called around to get more quotes from mechanics to fix her dead car. She was starting to feel guilty. She was starting to feel uncomfortable, as though he was doing too much for her.

She knew he had his past with gold-digging women, and that's why Amber always tried to make things equal between them. He wasn't allowed to take her anyplace fancy. If he bought her dinner, she bought him lunch the next day. She didn't want him buying her gifts, although she had accepted a brand-new box of high quality colored pencils and a new sketchbook from him because it had been so thoughtful.

She tried not to compare him to her ex. Because with Steven things had started out well, too. He bought her things and took her places, but soon those nice gestures became debts and he'd treated her as if she had owed him. Owed him all her time, owed him his way, owed him her obedience, and when she didn't give it to him, he became nasty and cold. And then one day she realized that she had asked him permission to go to the store.

She was a strong woman. She never thought that kind of thing could happen to her. She should have seen the warning signs in Steven. She should have known it was coming, but she didn't see a thing and that's what worried her about Chase.

"Hey."

She broke out of her thoughts to see him sitting on her front steps with a large bag at his side.

"Hey." She walked up to him. "What are you doing here? I thought I was going to see you tomorrow."

"You wouldn't let me pick you up from school and I really hated the thought of you on a bus at night alone."

"Millions of people do it every day, Chase," she said, feeling breathless at his sweetness.

"I know. But millions of people aren't crazy about you."

"Oh."

Damn. He was too good. Almost too perfect. There had to be something wrong. Something she wasn't seeing.

"What's in the bag?" she asked him, not wanting to think about what could be wrong when everything was feeling so right.

"Dinner. I made chicken piccata and there are some marbled marshmallow brownies for dessert."

"You made me dinner? You actually cooked?"

"My siblings aren't the only ones who can throw down in the kitchen. I just need a carefully laid out recipe."

She smiled. He was the first person in a long time who made her smile like this. "I'm glad you're here, Chase."

"I wouldn't have been able to sleep without seeing you tonight. How was your final?"

"It was tough, but I think I did pretty well, thanks to you."

"Not thanks to me. You are really intelligent. I've just been at it a little longer than you have."

"Will you stay tonight?"

He nodded. "Will you let me take you out tomorrow? There's a little art theater downtown that is showing old black-and-white films for a dollar. They've got food trucks lined up in front of it. I figured we could sample food from around the world."

"Of course, I'll go out with you tomorrow. It's the only thing I want to do."

Two evenings later Chase walked up to his parents' stately home in a beautiful old affluent section of Seattle. He had never thought about where he had come from until recently. But he'd always had everything. Every chance. Every opportunity. He worked incredibly hard and earned every penny, but he didn't have to. Things were just easier for him. He wondered who or where he'd be under different circumstances. Would he be like Amber, whose parents worked hard every single day of their lives but never had much money? Where would he be if his parents couldn't have afforded to send him to college? What would his life be like if he was faced with crippling student loan debt? Would he still be the same man he was now if he had been born to a different set of parents in a different part of town?

He didn't know the answer to any of those questions, but being with Amber made him think a lot about things lately. He was thankful for the life he had. He gave back, but he did that out of obligation more than anything else. He was truly appreciative of all that life had brought him, and he was especially appreciative that he had spent the past few weeks with a woman who kept his mind as active as his body.

The door opened before he had the chance to knock and he saw his beautiful mother standing before him wearing cream-colored designer slacks and a peach top that went perfectly with her brown skin. Her makeup was just right; there wasn't a strand of hair out of place. His entire life he had seen her that way. He wondered what she would look like with her hair mussed and clothes that came from a discount store instead of a pricey boutique. Would she still carry herself the same? Would she still walk around with that slight air of superiority that made her Nadia Drayson?

"Hello, son." She kissed his cheek. "You're late. You're never late."

"Am I?" He looked down at his watch and sure enough he was eleven minutes late to his monthly family dinner. "Oh, I apologize. I must have gotten caught up."

He had been with Amber. She had gone to kiss him goodbye and it had turned into more than just a little kiss.

"It's quite all right. Your cousin Belinda and her husband, Malik, are here visiting from Chicago. They are stopping over on their way to LA."

"That's nice." He was actually a little surprised to hear that his Chicago cousins were in his parents' home. He had no problem with them, but there had been some strain between the two branches of the family; it was almost a feud, going back to some ancient debt from a few generations ago. Chase liked to think of it as the Drayson cold war.

"Tonight we are having roasted pork tenderloin with a spicy blueberry reduction and creamy barley risotto."

"Spicy blueberry?"

"Your brother recommended it. It's turned out quite well."

"You made it, mother. I'm sure it did."

She smiled at him. "Don't tell the others, but you're my favorite."

"You tell them the same thing." He smiled back.

"I'm not sure what you are talking about. Graham, dear. Chase has arrived." He followed his mother into the living room to see his father with a glass of bourbon in his hand.

"Hello, son. I tried calling you the other day, but I couldn't reach you."

"Oh, really?" He made a practice of not answering calls when he was with Amber. He hadn't done that in other relationships. He always picked up his phone and answered his email. But now that he was with Amber, the less distraction he had from the outside world, the happier he was. "I'm sorry. I hope it wasn't important."

"Not terribly. I have a friend who would like you to look at his investment portfolio. I told him you were a financial genius."

"You give me too much credit, Dad."

"I don't. You have something special. Not everyone has your skill. I would hate to see it go to waste."

Chase knew that was a slight dig at him for taking a leave of absence from his job to work at the bakery. His mother didn't like that any of her children were involved in this venture, but their father seemed more amenable to it. That is, when it involved Jackson and Mariah. Chase was often held to a slightly different standard than his siblings. A higher one. Especially by his father, who pushed him always to be the best in everything that he attempted. It wasn't in a harsh or overzealous way, but there was just a little more weight on Chase, a little more pressure than the other two received.

"Hey, Chase." He turned to see his cousin Belinda and her husband, Malik, walk in with Jackson and Mariah. "We didn't know you had come in. We were just on the patio talking shop."

"Yes," Nadia said with a slight sigh. "Last bit of conversation I heard involved cupcakes. It's every mother's dream to hear her children discussing cupcake flavors after working so hard to make sure they have gotten the best education that money can offer."

"You say that, Mom, but you never turn down any of the treats I bring you from the bakery," Jackson said as he wrapped an arm around his mother.

"Well, of course not. That would just be rude."

Jackson grinned at her before he turned his attention to Chase. "I see you've made it. Finally pulled yourself away from that sexy girl of yours."

"Girl?" Nadia's eyes widened and Chase wanted to smack his brother. "Are you seeing someone, Chase? You didn't tell me you were seeing anyone."

"I am," he said, not wanting to discuss his love life in front of the entire family.

"Well, who is she?"

"Her name is Amber."

"Sweetheart, I think you know me well enough by now to know that when I ask who is she, you should tell me more than her name. I would like to know what she does, who her people are. What makes her anywhere near good enough to be with my firstborn son."

"She's my friend, Mom," Mariah spoke up. "I told you about her."

"The barista with the car trouble?" He could hear the disdain in his mother's voice. "Oh, Chase. I thought you would have learned from your mistakes. There is a certain type of woman that you don't get involved with, and one who is swimming in debt certainly qualifies as that type."

"She's more than a barista. She's a jewelry designer and a graduate student and, even if she weren't those things, who I see is my business."

"I think you might have to make it all of our business." Jackson plopped himself down on the couch. "He's crazy about this one, Mom. I went over there and there were cups on his coffee table without coasters and take-out containers from cheap places, and did you know that he called in sick to play hooky with her?"

"You done tattling?" Chase asked Jackson.

"I'm not tattling. I'm reporting and I'm all for you being with her. I like Amber and you're a little bit looser since she has been around. Plus she's outstanding to look at."

"If Jackson likes her," his mother said, "then that's a sure sign that she is all wrong for you. I'm just wondering how long it takes before she decides she is going to trap you. You are very eligible, son, and there are dozens of nice women that I approve of that would make perfectly lovely wives. I'm not sure why you are wasting time on this woman you have no future with."

"Can I say something?" Belinda asked as she looked between Chase and his mother. "You seem so dead set against Chase being with this woman, but I haven't heard a single reason why he shouldn't be."

"We live our lives a certain way. We travel in certain social circles. Even if you love this girl, can you really see her being your wife? Fitting in with your friends? We have that huge charity ball next month that I'm hosting. Will she be able to handle herself there? Keep up with conversations? Be able to speak eloquently about current affairs?"

"She isn't some trash I picked up on the street and put some polish on. She's a smart, talented woman. She teaches a class for underprivileged girls at a community center and she values education. She doesn't just throw money at a problem—she works to change things."

"She can't throw money at a problem if she doesn't have any," his mother retorted.

"She is talented, Mom," Mariah spoke up, defending her friend. "Look." She took off the bracelet Chase had given her and showed it to her mother. "Amber made this. She sells them in a few boutiques around the city. She's talented."

"It's cute," Nadia said dismissively. "And I'm sure she's a nice person if all of my children seem to like her, but I just don't think she's right for Chase." She patted his cheek. "I'm going to see about dinner."

Chase repressed a sigh, knowing that there was no winning with his mother. He liked Amber. He didn't give a damn what anyone in his family thought. He would be with her. But he did wonder about the long term. If his mother didn't like her, she wouldn't make things easy for Amber. And Amber seemed uncomfortable with wealth, and his parents never had a problem showing theirs.

How would she fit in at family functions and charity balls? How would she function in a world that she didn't like to travel in? She might not want to be a part of this. They were similar creatures, but there was still a world of things separating them.

"Let me pour you a drink, son. You look like you need it," Graham said as he walked away from him and toward his decanter.

Malik walked up to him, placing a supportive hand on his shoulder. "I started out driving the bakery delivery truck. I worked with Belinda at the bakery before I started The Brothers Who Bake blog and wrote the cookbook. Go ahead and be happy with your barista. Her past doesn't dictate your future. Just be happy. The rest of the world be damned."

He nodded. Malik had a great point.

Chapter 11

"What do you think about cheesy apple-pie cupcakes?" Chase asked Amber that next evening as they strolled hand in hand in Myrtle Edwards Park as the sun was just setting.

Amber barely heard his question. She had been so focused on the beauty of the scenery around her, the feel of his big hand in hers and the rush of feelings that came over her when he looked at her. The sky was a beautiful purply orange and there were brightly colored blossoms lining the paths. Elliott Bay was the perfect place to see views of Puget Sound, the Olympic Mountains and Mount Rainier. She had never been here before, thinking that this part of town was a place that only tourists ever went, but Chase had surprised her with this trip after she was finished teaching her class.

It would have been easy for him to take her to a fancy restaurant. It would have been easy for him to take her on those typical dates men like him usually went on, but he seemed to go out of his way to find things that she might enjoy.

He found black-and-white films at a movie theater that still served real butter on their popcorn and the art exhibit featuring women over fifty. He found little hole-in-the-wall restaurants that served good, filling, cheap food. He was trying with her, trying to do things that would make her happy.

Sometimes it made her feel guilty that maybe he was missing out on things that he wanted to do, places that he wanted to try, all because she didn't want him spending a lot of money on her. She wanted a relationship of equals, but she wondered how long he would be interested in someone whose lifestyle was so different from his.

"Did you say an apple-pie and cheese cupcake?"

"I did. I hear that people in the Midwest enjoy apple pie with a slice of cheddar cheese."

"Oh, sweetheart, that's the most original thing I have ever heard."

"Do you think it will taste bad?"

"I honestly don't know. We can try to make them. Although the last attempt didn't turn out too well."

"We burned them because you put icing on my face and the next thing I remember was licking it off your stomach."

"We should bake more together," she said, returning the hot look he gave her.

"Maybe we shouldn't. Next time we'll burn something down." He laughed and shook his head. "I wished I was more like my siblings. They know what flavors go together and they can think of forty different things that might work, and I keep thinking about how much it would cost to make each cupcake and the price we would have to sell it for to make a decent profit."

"I think you're thinking too hard about it. Just relax and it will come to you. I promise."

"Are you saying I'm uptight?"

"Only sometimes, sweetheart." She kissed his cheek. "When it really matters you aren't uptight at all. My toes curl thinking about all the ways you aren't uptight when we are alone."

He paused and looked at her. His eyes drinking in her face, like they often did, making her feel beautiful. "Let me take you away for a weekend. Somewhere nice."

"I can't afford to go away right now."

"Your paying for the trip would defeat the purpose of me taking you away, wouldn't it?"

She blinked at him. "Oh. I…" She wanted to go. She wanted to just say yes and spend a few days away from it all with him, not worrying about money or her car or her grad school grades. But she was torn. She knew it would make him happy if she just relented, but she didn't want him doing any more for her than he had already done. Him just being there when she got home was enough. It made her happy.

She hadn't wanted a relationship. She had sworn off men until she had finished grad school, made some more headway into her business. But he had snuck in when she least expected it. "It's not the right time. Maybe in a month or so," she said not wanting to commit, but not wanting to hurt him, either.

He shook his head. "I have the feeling it's never going to be the right time."

"What does that mean?"

"It means what it means. I feel like I don't have you yet."

"I wasn't aware that I was property to be owned."

"I didn't mean it like that." She could see that he was annoyed with her and she was waiting for the coldness to come, the nasty remark, the cut, and she braced herself for it. But it never came. In fact he was silent for so long the lack of words was almost more painful than if he had hurled an insult at her.

"Say something," she said when the silence became too much.

"I don't know what it's going to take for you to trust me, but I'm going to keep being here for you and keep caring about you until you let me in. I won't stop until I get there because you are worth it to me."

"You do too much for me as it is. I don't want you to think you have to take care of me."

"I don't think that. But I want to take care of you. I want to solve all your problems and relieve all your stress. I want to buy you things and take you places and be there when you go to sleep and be the first person you see when you wake up. There's something about you and I don't know what it is, but it's something I'm not willing to give up on."

The air left her lungs and she knew right then and

there that she had fallen all the way and absolutely in love with him. There was nothing she could do about it and that's what scared her the most.

"How's the cupcake bite coming along?" Jackson asked Chase as they stood off to the side in the bakery just watching the action going on. Foot traffic had been lighter than normal these past couple of days. Chase had learned that other bakeries had started duplicating the Draynut, but sales hadn't gone down, thankfully, with 87 percent of customers who walked through their doors between eight and ten coming out with Mariah's original pastry creation.

There were many imitators but only one origina-tor, but he knew that if they didn't start to launch new products soon, interest was going to wane. "It's com-ing along. I've got some ideas."

"You keep saying that." Jackson shook his head. "Let's hear them."

"Amber's been helping me sort through them. Not many of them have been approved."

"Really?" He grinned. "Give me one that she said no to."

"Lemon pumpkin surprise."

"Lemon pumpkin? What exactly is the surprise?"

"Lemon curd filling."

"Pumpkin and lemon curd? I don't know about that. It might be able to work with a lemon cream cheese icing. Have you played with the recipe?"

"No. We attempted one recipe. It didn't end well. I'm surprised you aren't laughing at me."

"Why would I laugh at you for that? I'm trying to prefect a bacon pancake cupcake. If I know one thing about you, it's that you take every assignment given to you seriously. Even if it is just coming up with a cupcake flavor. If you want we can do some test kitchen stuff at my place. I'm trying to figure out the right consistency for the cupcake. I don't want it to be too dense."

"I'm a little surprised at you, Jackson. I knew you were a food snob, but I never thought you would take owning a bakery so seriously. Half the time I keep waiting for you to tell me you're selling out."

"Nah." He shook his head. "This is a family business. I would never sell my share. We're in this for better or for worse."

"Speaking of for better or for worse..." Chase gripped his younger brother's arm, not sure he was seeing things clearly. "I think that is our mother walking through the door."

"Mom?" Jackson shook his head. "No. It must be someone who looks like her."

But sure enough their mother did walk through the door and toward them, decked out in designer clothes with her hair twisted up elegantly.

"Mom?" Jackson stepped forward and gently reached out to touch her cheek. "Is that you?"

"Don't be silly, Jackson. Of course it's me."

"Forgive him, Mom," Chase said. "But we're just surprised to see you in here."

She looked around the bakery with her critical eye. "Is there something wrong with wanting to visit my children and see how they are?"

"No, but you don't like it here," Jackson said looking slightly on edge. "In fact this place is the bane of your existence."

"Don't be so dramatic. It's just that my brilliant, highly educated children decided to throw away their educations and futures to work in an unstable bakery. A mother gets a little touchy about those things."

"We are not throwing away our educations, Mother," Chase said, defending his actions to her once again. "Between the Draynut and Myers Coffee Roasters we are bringing in a steady, stable stream of customers that won't be trailing off anytime soon. Plus we are operating in the black and have made a fifteen percent profit this month. We are planning on rolling out new products in the coming months and, according to my projections, we can grow our business up to twenty-five percent."

"You see, Mom." Jackson puffed his chest up a bit. "Nobody is throwing away their education. We're using what we learned to make this business successful. You need to have a little faith in us."

"You're my children. I believe you can do anything. You wouldn't be my children if you couldn't, but I just worry. Your father worked his way up from nothing so that we could give you every opportunity in the world. We just don't ever want to see you in a position where you are in need. And just the thought of this place not working out keeps me up at night."

"Mom, we're all right," Chase said, affectionately squeezing her arm. "Even if this place goes down in flames, which it won't, we'll be all right. You know that I have always planned for my future."

He saw Amber out of the corner of his eye. She was chatting with an older customer as she carried her mug and what looked like a cream-and-jam-filled biscuit over to her table. She didn't have to do that. There was no waitstaff at the bakery but Amber always took the extra time with their customers. He loved that about her. She was thoughtful and kind and always did just a little bit more than she had to.

"Excuse me, son. I always prided myself on my conversation skills, but maybe I need to brush up on them if you are having such a hard time focusing on this one."

"It's Amber," Jackson said.

Chase made a soft noise of agreement. Amber was walking past them, probably on her way to clock out for the day. He knew she wasn't going to stop. The most she did was give him soft shy smile or little private looks. She tried to keep it as professional as possible at work, and normally he would agree that workplace romances should be conducted discreetly and quietly, but this time he didn't give a damn who knew.

He grasped her arm, his body warming as soon as it came into contact with her soft skin. "Come here a moment." He tucked her smaller body into his own, and she snuggled into him as though it was natural, as if her body was designed to do that when it came into contact with his.

"Hello, sir."

"Hello, miss. You done for today?"

"I am. Just about to head over to the community center. One of the other instructors is going to pick me up."

"I won't keep you. I just wanted you to meet my mother."

"Oh." She stood up straight and smoothed her clothes, looking adorably flustered. "It's nice to meet you, Mrs. Drayson. I'm Amber. Please excuse my appearance."

Compared to his pristine mother, Amber looked rumpled. Hell, anyone would have looked rumpled compared to his mother, but he preferred Amber's wild curls and her funky earrings and how her beauty was always so effortless. He didn't think he would like her all sleek and smooth. Amber didn't tick off any of the boxes on that long list of things he had thought he wanted in a woman, but she made him happy.

"I've heard a lot about you, Amber. My son speaks highly of you."

"Does he?" She looked up at him. "I didn't know he spoke of me at all."

"All of my children like you. It's rare they all agree on something so wholeheartedly."

"I'm one of four. I know how it is." She smiled shyly. "Chase has told me all about your charity work. Have you ever considered taking on a mentee or teaching a class? There are so many girls out there who could benefit from learning from you. We're always looking for successful women down at the center."

"The center?"

"I teach at the Gwendolyn Brooks Center for Excellence. I'm teaching the young women in my class how to run a small business as well as the art of jewelry design, but I would love for a woman with more experience to come talk to them."

Chase watched as his mother's face remained neutral, not giving away what she was thinking. He would give a million dollars to know what was going on in her head. His mother always helped out charities, but at this stage in her life she was more of a planner and less of a doer. She wouldn't actually get her hands dirty. "Hit up people for volunteering later." He stroked his thumb across Amber's cheek. "You've got to get going now."

"You're right!" She glanced at her watch. "It was very nice meeting you, Mrs. Drayson." She shook her hand. "Jackson, we'll talk more about the boys' cooking class."

"I'll call you tonight."

"Goodbye, handsome." She kissed Chase's cheek.

"Goodbye, gorgeous." He caught her chin between his fingers and kissed her mouth, just a little longer than he should have with his mother and brother standing there.

She blushed, a slightly embarrassed smile crossing her face. "It was lovely to meet you, Mrs. Drayson. Feel free to ignore what I said before. I forget myself sometimes."

"It was a pleasure, dear," his mother said politely. Amber gave them all one last wave before she was off, leaving the three of them alone again.

"She's one of those do-gooder types, isn't she?" Nadia said after a moment.

"Yes. She is."

"She's quite lovely. Beautiful skin. What did you say her parents did?"

"Her father is a court officer and her mother is a trained seamstress."

"Hmm. Bring her for dinner next month." She kissed both of her sons' cheeks and turned to leave.

"Did what I think happened just happen?" Jackson stared after their mother, kind of bewildered.

"Yeah." Chase couldn't believe it himself. His mother had just given Amber her stamp of approval.

Chapter 12

Amber heard Chase's heavy footsteps come down the hallway and toward her workroom. Her heart beat a little faster, even though she should be annoyed about his interrupting her. She was a little behind on some pieces she had been commissioned to make. Plus she had a meeting with the owner of a specialty jewelry store that only sold pieces from up-and-coming designers. It was an important meeting. One that could be a huge advance in her career if her jewelry was carried there. That's why she needed this time to work, but still she wanted to see Chase.

"Hey." He peeked his head in. "I just wanted to bring you a little snack before I left."

Damn, he was sweet. She wondered how he had gone

so long unmarried. Any woman would be lucky to have him as her husband. "Come in."

He had a plate of assorted veggies and hummus in his hand. "It's brain food." He set the plate on the side table and knelt before her, taking her hands in his. "Don't work too long tonight."

"You're leaving?" They had spent nearly every night together, switching back and forth between her place and his. She had gotten used to falling asleep wrapped in his arms and waking up with a kiss on her forehead.

"I know you have work to do, and I feel like I'm bothering you."

"You weren't. You aren't."

"I want to bother you, though. The temptation to come back here every five minutes is getting to be overwhelming."

"I like having you here. It is a distraction because I wonder what you're doing out there while I'm in here, but truthfully I would be just as distracted if you were home. I'm not sure what exactly you have done to me, Chase Drayson, but my head has been all filled up with you."

He lifted her hands to his mouth and kissed both of them. "What are you working on?"

She picked up her sketchbook and showed him a drawing of the piece she was creating. "It's a neckpiece made with fourteen-karat gold and freshwater pearls. It's one of my more extravagant pieces. It goes with these." She lifted the delicate pair of pearl flower earrings that she had painstakingly made last night. "I'm going to show them to the owner of the jewelry store

I'm meeting with. I need to show that I can do high-end and mass-market pieces."

"They are beautiful, Amber. I would never have believed that someone could make these by hand. You're going to be successful. I know it."

"Thank you." She pressed her lips to his forehead, letting them linger there, not sure how to tell him that she didn't want him to go. He should go home. She needed to work, but she didn't want to be left alone in this apartment tonight.

"My firm is throwing a party at the Burke Museum tomorrow night. Would you want to come with me?"

"Oh, baby, I've got so much work to do on this piece. Is it an important function?"

"Nah." He looked disappointed. "I know I sprung this on you last minute. I just wanted to show off my new girlfriend to my old friends. Don't worry about it."

She felt guilty. Lower than low. He didn't ask her for much. He didn't ask her for anything. But she had so much work to do and she had been spending so much time with him that she was letting the other really important parts of her life slide.

Finishing her degree and becoming a successful jewelry designer were the most important things to her. She hadn't meant to fall in love. She didn't have time to. "I'm so sorry, Chase."

"Don't be." He kissed her cheek. "I'm proud of you. I don't know another woman who could do everything that you do and do it so well. You amaze me every day."

He couldn't have made her feel worse if he had called her every nasty name there was out there. He was too sweet to her and she didn't know what to say so she kissed him. She cupped his face in her hands and kissed him slowly, sliding her tongue deeply into his mouth. He let out a low moan and that's all it took to heat things up.

She pulled his shirt from his pants, undoing the buttons as fast as she could so that she could feel his skin. She loved his chest, how broad and hard and smooth it was. She loved the way it felt when he was on top of her. Chest to chest. Skin to skin. Her nipples tightened in anticipation of feeling it again.

He pulled away from her and stood up, breathing heavily. There was slight surprise in his eyes combined with pure lust. And he ripped his shirt away from his body, kicking off his shoes. His hands reached for the button on his pants, but she pushed his hands away, wanting to do it herself. Wanting to reveal him in her own way.

He hissed out a slow breath when she pulled him out. Sliding her lips along his shaft, she left behind little wet kisses. She noticed his fist clench and unclench, his hands shaking slightly as she drove him a little wilder. She loved doing this with Chase. Teasing him. Working him up. He liked to be in charge in bed. He liked to spend hours pleasing her body. Kissing her from head to toe and starting all over again.

He was the best lover she had ever had and she was glad that she got to experience him, but she wanted to give to him, too. She wanted to make him feel good. She wanted to imprint herself on his memory so even long after they parted he would think of her the way she knew she would think of him.

She slid the head into her mouth, sucking in that way she knew nearly undid him. He grunted, his control slipping. She cupped his testicles as she worked, seeing how far she could push him before he would break.

He cursed. He moaned her name. He turned her on. And before she could process what was happening he pushed her away, pulling her out of her chair and onto her feet. He yanked at the bottom of her tank top.

"Take it off," he ordered. She did, her excitement growing as she watched him rip off his pants.

He came at her, tugging down her bra straps and pushing the whole thing to her waist. He moaned again as he stared at her. She wondered how she looked to him, her breasts bared, her hair wild and only a little pair of cotton shorts separating them. He ran his hands over her breasts, stroking them, touching her nipples, tugging on them slightly, the tiny bit of pain only heightening her pleasure. He dipped his head to take her in his mouth. The feeling was too good and her knees gave out. He caught her, scooping her up and carrying her to the small bed she kept in the room.

"I can't wait anymore," he panted. Before she knew what was happening, her shorts were gone and he was on top of her, pushing inside her, filling her up, making her feel fulfilled.

"Don't hold back." She wrapped her legs around him, taking even more of him in. "I want all of you."

He granted her wish. His tempo was fast and furious and she wanted to keep her eyes open, to see his face when he pumped inside of her, but it was too amazing and all she could do was shut her eyes and experience him. He had learned her body. He knew what she liked better than she did. He kissed her throat and called out her name and said sweet, beautiful, nonsensical things that she didn't understand but wanted to hear more of.

"You're too good, Amber. You're too good," he said into her ear. His pace changed, his thrusts became quicker, harder. She dug her fingers into his back, feeling her climax coming on.

"I can't hold on any longer. Please come for me, Amber."

She wanted to give him everything he asked for. She wanted to give him the world, but she knew if she couldn't, she could at least give him this. Her orgasm was powerful, causing her to cry out, causing tears to form in her eyes and roll down her cheeks. Sex with him always managed to move her.

"What's the matter?" He removed himself from inside her and took her face in his hands. "Did I hurt you?"

"Of course not." She wrapped her arms around him and hugged him tightly to her. It only hurt to love him this much. "That was…" She didn't have words to describe what they had just done. "Thank you."

"I know how you feel." He kissed the side of her face. "This is something special, isn't it?"

It was. She didn't think that love like this was possible.

The finance firm Chase worked for always gave extravagant parties for their clients twice a year, to thank everyone for their faith in them and their hard work and to basically show the world that they could afford to throw parties filled with expensive champagne and lobster appetizers. The downtown Seattle museum was the perfect setting for an event like this. The space was huge and elegantly decorated. The perfect location to attract wealthy new clients who were patrons of the arts. Normally Chase would be working the room, making connections, brokering new deals, but he didn't care about any of that stuff tonight. There was one thing that his eyes kept focusing on and she was sipping a glass of champagne. He couldn't stop looking at her. He didn't want to stop looking at her. She wore a golden bandage dress over her curvy body, and it looked like heaven against her skin—that combined with her wild curls and her gorgeous face made her the best-looking woman in the room, but she could have worn a sack and Chase would have thought the same thing. He almost regretted asking her to come to this party. He could have spent the night alone with her at her place or his. They could have been laughing over some silly television show or brainstorming cupcake ideas or just doing nothing together.

But he'd asked her to come here and she had. And selfishly he didn't want to share her with the world.

"Stop looking at me like that." Amber gave him a sexy smile. "I can practically see your thoughts."

"I can't help myself. You're the sexiest woman in the room. How does it feel to be the sexiest person everywhere you go?"

"It's a trial, really. More of a cross to bear than anything." She grinned at him as she put her champagne down and looped her arms around his neck. "I'm going to start a support group for sexy people. But seriously, I think you're only saying that because I let you see me naked."

"I thought you were the sexiest woman in the room even before I saw you naked."

"Oh, really? You had a hard time remembering my name. I couldn't have left too much of an impression on you."

He leaned in to kiss her and he had to make sure to keep his arousal in check. Memories of last night flooded his brain. The sex was more than amazing. It was emotional and powerful and made him feel raw. "I'm crazy about you, Amber." But truthfully he was more than just crazy about her. He was in love with her. He wanted to tell her, but he knew it was too soon. It was crazy to fall in love with someone so soon, but it was love.

"You're too good to me, Chase." She rested her head on his shoulder.

"I'm glad you ended up coming tonight."

"Am I holding my own with your friends?"

"Of course. Were you afraid you wouldn't?" He had been afraid of that before. Afraid she wouldn't fit in with his life and his friends, but that was his mother putting those thoughts in his head. She was smart and insightful and made him see things in a different way. Even if she couldn't hold her own in this room of people he would still feel the same way about her.

"I don't know. Maybe. It was important for you to have me here. I didn't want to disappoint you."

"You didn't disappoint me." He stroked his thumb across her cheek. "You can't as long as you are yourself."

She leaned closer to kiss him and as soon as her lips pressed his he felt a hand land on his shoulder.

"Hey, Drayson. Heard you were here." He looked up to see one of the senior partners in his firm.

"Hello, Robert. How are you?"

"I'm fine. I see that you are better than me, judging by the way you can't seem to pull yourself away from your lovely companion."

"This is my girlfriend, Amber Bernard. Amber, this is Robert Kelly, one of the senior partners at my firm."

"It's nice to meet you."

"Thank you. You, as well. I hope you're trying to convince Chase to come back to us full-time. He's on track to make partner. The man should be making millions every day. Not worrying about crullers and such things."

Amber glanced at Chase before she looked back to Robert. "I'm a firm believer in doing what makes you happy, Mr. Kelly, and if being a partner in your firm will make Chase happy, then he should do it."

"I agree." He nodded with a grin. "And that's why I have come over here. I think I have a few ways to make Chase happy at our firm. Would you mind if I stole him away for a moment?"

"Of course not."

Chase put his hand on her arm, reluctant to leave her alone at this large party. "You going to be okay?"

"I'll be terribly afraid without you." She grinned at him. "Go. I'll be fine."

He nodded and walked away with his boss, remembering what his life had been like before he had been at the bakery. Long days, lonely nights, work hours that neared eighty a week. He'd thought he was content, making a great salary, moving up the ranks of his company, but he hadn't been happy. These past few weeks he had been happy with Amber, and he didn't think there was anything his boss could say that would make him jeopardize that.

Chapter 13

Amber studied the wall-sized painting that was displayed at the museum. It was a green square on a white canvas. Just a green square on white canvas. She had gone to art school and studied the greats, but she'd never understood modern art like this. It looked like something her little cousin could have done. But she would never admit that aloud. It would make her lose serious street cred with her art school classmates.

"I heard that the green represents an island that the artist felt he was on, and the whiteness is the loneliness surrounding him," a man said from behind her.

Amber didn't have to turn around to know who was speaking to her. She knew the voice. She had spent two years of her life listening to nearly everything that he said.

"Steven." She steeled herself before she faced him. He was a handsome man. He always had been, but there was an extra air of maturity floating around him. He was dressed in his signature all black, but his hair had gone white at the temples and in his beard, giving him a distinguished salt-and-pepper look. But unlike the younger girl she'd been when she met him, she didn't get butterflies in her stomach. She'd thought she might feel anger when she saw him, or hurt, but she only felt foolish because she had let him rule her life for so long.

"You are looking amazing."

"Thank you." She turned back to look at the painting, done with the conversation.

"Aren't you going to ask me how I've been or what I'm doing here?"

How had *he* been? What was *he* doing there? He was still all about him all the time. It was almost nice to see that nothing had changed.

"I'm not going to ask." She wandered to the next exhibit on display. A large gothic piece, but she could barely concentrate on it because he had followed her. She could feel his eyes on her back.

"I'm surprised to see you at an event like this. When we were together it was like pulling teeth to get you out of the house and away from your little jewelry collection."

Little jewelry collection. The condescending words struck her in the chest, but she said nothing, refusing to give Steven the satisfaction of knowing that he had gotten to her.

"But I guess when you're with a man like Chase

Drayson, real art and culture become more of a priority."

"Excuse me?" She quickly turned around to face him.

"What's the matter? You're surprised I know who your new man is? Everybody who is anybody knows who the Draysons are. They are prominent members of the community. I'm just surprised that he's here with you. Maybe I'm not. Chase has been known to date women who are after his money and status."

"Are you suggesting that I am one of those women?"

"Am I saying you're a gold digger? No. But I do know that it must be getting tiresome working in a coffee shop and paying for grad school on your own."

She ignored the implication, holding on to her temper by a thread. "How did you know I was in grad school?"

"We still have mutual friends."

"You were asking about me. Does it bother you that I continued to better myself after we broke up?"

"You could have bettered yourself when you were with me," he said sharply.

She stiffened slightly at his tone, memories of their last year together flooding her. "I'm better without you." She stood taller, forced herself to look him in the eye even though she saw disdain there.

"Better? You call hanging off a rich man better? Don't you think he knows your end game?"

"There is no end game. I want nothing from Chase. I haven't taken a cent or gift from him."

"You don't have to get all self-righteous with me. I understand. It's easy to see why you would latch onto him. You're not dumb. You realized that the jewelry-making was just a hobby and that grad school is a waste of time. Chase Drayson is your way out of all that mess. You know if you settle down with him that you'll be set for life. But, baby girl, you should probably know that a man like him is never really going to marry a woman like you. You should know that he wouldn't want you to be the mother of his children. He needs someone on his level."

"And what level would that be?" She clenched her fists to stop her hands from shaking.

"You know. You're just not on it. But don't worry. Neither am I. Not yet at least. That's why we were good together. We could lift each other up. Especially if you have decided that your role should be that of wife and mother."

"You used to dazzle me," she said calmly. "When I was still a girl I thought you were worldly and so-phisticated and had everything going for you. But I've grown up since then and all I see you as now is a needy, pathetic excuse for a man, who can only lift himself up while tearing others down. I actually feel sorry for you. I do know my role. My role is to finish my MBA. My role is to make my business a success. My role is supporting myself and to not let any man think he has any sort of hold over me. And your role… Your role is to get out of my face before I smash yours into one of these very expensive paintings."

"Is there a problem here?" She heard Chase's voice behind her.

She turned to face him and her heart leaped as her

stomach sank. He looked so dashing in his evening wear. So like he belonged here when all evening she had felt out of place, like a poseur. As though she was pretending to fit in.

She loved him. She was in love with him. But how long could the finance guru and the poor jewelry designer really be together? She'd known when she started things up with him that they had an expiration date stamped on them.

"There's no problem here. Amber and I were just catching up."

"Really?" Chase stepped closer and wrapped his arm around her. "It seems to me that Amber requested that you leave her sight. If you don't get the hell out of here, I will make sure you follow her request."

"You're threatening to call security on me?"

"Who said anything about security? I'm threatening to kick your ass." He looked down at Amber. "I thought I was pretty clear. What do you think, baby?"

"You were perfectly clear."

"Fine. Goodbye, Amber." Steven stomped away.

Chase watched him go, shaking his head. "Are you okay?" He kissed her forehead.

"I am." She leaned into him, taking comfort in his closeness. "I'm just a little hot."

"Come on. I know a place where you can cool off."

He led her to the dimly lit atrium, which was nearly breathtaking in its beauty. It was filled with lush, green trees and little gurgling ponds with elegant water features. Chase led her to a bench in front of the koi-filled pond and for a moment all Amber could do was watch the colorful fish swim in circles.

"Who was that guy?"

"A nobody."

"A nobody wouldn't make you want to smash his face." He took her chin between his fingers. "Should I be embarrassed to admit that seeing you threaten that guy turned me on?"

She grinned at him. "You're not very hard to turn on."

"Only when it comes to you. Tell me who that man was."

"My ex."

"Oh," he said after a moment. "I think it might be time to tell me about him."

"It's over. That's all that's important. I don't really want to talk about him." She didn't want to talk about him, but she kept thinking about what he'd said. He accused her of being a gold digger, of using Chase. She knew if Steven thought that about her, then other people were probably thinking the same thing. The truth was, she wasn't on Chase's level. They weren't in the same places in their lives and the last thing she wanted to be thought of as was needy, as someone who needed a man to get by. As someone who needed to be supported instead of treated as an equal partner.

She had already set aside some of her needs to be with him. It wasn't his fault. He hadn't asked her to, but he was a distraction. She thought about him instead of the next step in her plan. She spent time with him instead of working on her jewelry.

She loved him, but he wasn't her goal. And when she left her last relationship she'd made a promise to herself never to choose love over her dreams. She didn't want to be like her mother, who gave up so much for so many others. She didn't want to look back on life and have any regrets. She didn't want to wonder what if...

She felt Chase's lips brush over her cheek. "Tell me what's going on in that head of yours. I can see so much in your eyes."

"I love you," she said, the words just kind of slipping out. "I didn't mean to fall in love with you. It's too soon. It's too crazy."

"It's not."

She looked up at him. "It's too much for me."

"What?"

"I can't afford to fall in love right now. I had this plan, Chase. These goals, and falling in love with you wasn't a part of them."

He shook his head. "What are you saying?"

"That I love you, but I'm not ready for a relationship right now."

"You have one conversation with your ex and you're ready to throw out what we have?"

It was Amber's turn to shake her head. "I'm not really sure what we have."

He looked hurt by her words. She hadn't meant to hurt him, but she could see it plainly on his face.

"You know this is real, and special. You know you have never felt this way about anybody before. I know how you feel because I feel it in you when I kiss you, when I touch you, when I talk to you. I'm not sure about many things that don't have to do with numbers, but I'm sure of this. Of us."

"Chase." Her throat burned. Her vision became blurry, but holding back tears proved impossible. "This is already hard as it is. Please, don't make this harder for me."

"I'm not making it hard. You're the one who is giving up on a good thing."

"I love you." She kissed his cheek and then ran off, unable to stand how much she had just hurt him.

She'd walked away from him. Chase couldn't believe Amber had just walked away from him last night. One conversation with her ex and she decided she didn't want to be with him anymore.

It felt as though someone had shot him in the chest. He wasn't sure why he was surprised, though. She had always been the one to keep distance between them. There was always something blocking him from being with her completely. From loving her the way he wanted to. From loving her the way she deserved to be loved.

He tried to call her, to talk to her, to reason with her, but his calls had gone unanswered, and frankly he wasn't sure why he bothered. He had done all the chasing in this relationship and he was tired.

He didn't need to be with anyone who didn't want to be with him.

As he walked through the back door of the bakery, Jackson came out of his office. "Whoa. What happened to you?"

"Nothing." Chase walked past him and into his own

office, shutting the door. He didn't want to be bothered with anyone today. He just needed one last look at the numbers before he created a report listing the expenses they would generate for the upcoming Bite of Seattle.

"Don't tell me nothing is wrong." Jackson barged into his office. "You never wear jeans to work and while you're never really all that pleasant, you don't usually act like somebody ran over your dog. What happened?"

"Nothing. Get out. I'm working."

"It's Amber, isn't it?"

Chase looked up at his brother, the lie ready on his lips, but he couldn't bring himself to do it. "It's over."

"Why?"

"You'll have to ask her why."

"Fix it. She's good for you. You need her in your life."

"I didn't break it. I can't fix it." He shook his head, not feeling like discussing her anymore. "I have to get back to work, Jackson." He booted up his computer. "We've got a lot to prepare for with the Bite of Seattle coming up. I need to know the marketing budget and supplies that need to be ordered if we are going to be selling the new products there. You and Mariah are going to have to get together and come up with some estimates. Plus I'll need to know the layout of our booth so I can instruct the crew."

"So it's going to go back to this?"

"To what?" He looked up from his computer screen.

"To you working all the time. To you not having anything to say that doesn't have to do with numbers."

"I have to think about all of this stuff. You can't expect me to leave all the practical things to you and

Mariah. You all are too busy dreaming up new cake ideas. Somebody has to do the real work."

Jackson went quiet for a moment. His body stiffening. "I'm going to let you take that back," he said quietly. "I'm going to let you take that back because I know you are mad that your girl broke up with you. And I know that you really appreciate the amount of work Mariah and I do around here, running the front of the house and making our guests feel at home. Because if it were up to you, we would have a cold, sterile place with vending machines serving third-rate crap."

"Hey!" Anger tore through his stomach. "Don't—"

"I won't hold your comments against you," Jackson said, cutting him off. "I know how much you liked her. I know this must be hard."

"It came out of nowhere," he admitted.

"What happened?"

"I don't know. I took her to a work function last night and her ex was there. They exchanged words, and the next thing I knew I was going home alone. She won't even talk to me about what happened."

"Do you think she still loves him?"

"I don't know, but I would be a fool to go after a woman who was in love with another man."

Jackson nodded. "You would be. But I also think you would be a fool to give that woman up without a fight."

Chapter 14

Amber wasn't scheduled to work the day after she broke up with Chase and she was grateful for the day off because she didn't think she could face him. She didn't think she could see his face and hear his voice and stay strong.

She needed to achieve her goals and being tied down to a man wasn't a part of the plan. Although walking around with her broken heart wasn't good for her business, either. Without Chase, she would have more time to work on the pieces for her new collection. She had planned to finish the large neck piece she had been working on and start a new set of bracelets, but she just couldn't concentrate. Her mind wandered to Chase a thousand times. She kept hearing his words.

You're the one who is giving up on a good thing.

She kept seeing his face. How hurt he looked. How bewildered he was by her wish. He had called twice and each time she wanted to pick up the phone. She wanted to tell him that she'd made a mistake. But it wasn't really a mistake. She had to follow her dreams. She would end up hating herself if she didn't.

There was a knock at the door and her heart jumped into her throat.

Chase.

She hated that she got so excited at the thought of seeing him. She hated it because she knew it was going to be nearly impossible to get over him quickly. She thought about ignoring the door, but it would be foolish not to answer it. She was going to have to see him sooner or later, and she was scheduled to work that afternoon. She was actually closing tonight.

She wondered if he would be there late again, writing up reports, studying the numbers. She wondered if he would sit in that same dimly lit spot of the bakery with the top button of his shirt open, so engrossed in what he was doing that he didn't notice that he wasn't alone.

She wondered if somebody else would take her place and bring him a snack and some coffee to keep him going on those long nights.

She desperately hoped no one took her place. She hoped no one had little private conversations with him. She hoped no one saw the side of himself that he didn't often show the world. She knew that was selfish, but she loved him. And she didn't want anybody else loving him like she did.

She finally made her way from her workroom to the

front door to find her mother standing there instead of the tall beautiful brown-skinned man that she couldn't stop thinking about.

"Mama?" She shook her head, surprised to see her. "Did I forget you were coming?"

"Is that your polite way of suggesting I call before I come over?"

"No. It's—it's just that I'm surprised to see you here."

"I came to see my baby." She kissed her cheek. "I couldn't stop thinking about you today."

"Please come in. I'll fix us some lunch."

"No, you won't. I'll be the one doing the fixing." She headed directly to the kitchen and began pulling out the ingredients for grilled cheese with bacon and tomato. One of Amber's favorites.

Amber was tempted to tell her not to go to the trouble, but she was glad her mother was here. She could use some comforting mom food right now.

"How are you, baby girl?" her mother asked as she placed a healthy pat of butter in a pan.

"I'm fine," she lied as she came to stand next to her mom. "I meant to call and ask you how your class was going. Are you loving it?"

"I am. A lot has changed since I began illustrating. The technology alone makes one's head spin, but I'm keeping up. I'm learning so much."

"I'm so happy to hear that."

"Good." She assembled the sandwich and placed it in the hot pan. "Now are you going to tell me how you really are, or are we going to pretend like you haven't been crying?"

"What?"

"Your eyes are puffy. I'm your mother. You think I can't tell when there is something bothering you?"

"I've fallen in love," she blurted out.

Her mother was silent for a moment and then nodded. "With Chase? I would have fallen in love with him, too. Why does that scare you?"

"It's barely been a month. I have no business falling in love with anyone. Much less falling in love this hard."

"That's the thing about love. It sneaks up on you when you least expect it. You think I wanted to fall in love with your father? Of course not. He was working in a supermarket when I met him and I had all these big dreams." She flipped over the sandwich. "I was going to illustrate for all these big magazines. Draw political cartoons for the *Times*. But love knocked me right on my behind and being with your father seemed to take precedence over everything else."

That's what she was afraid of. Chase was the type of man who swept you off your feet and made you forget yourself. She didn't want to forget herself. She had done that once. She didn't want to do that again. "It's not the right time for me to fall in love."

"But is Chase the right guy, honey? I think he may be. I spoke to him on the phone last week."

"You did?"

"He answered your phone to say that you were busy with your new collection and didn't want to be disturbed, and we had a little chat. He's a sweet man. Thoughtful. I like him a lot."

"You liked him even before you spoke to him."

"It was the look in your eyes when you spoke of him. Any man who can make you look like that must be something. But then I spoke to him and knew he was something. He's crazy about you, Amber. He's so different from your last fellow."

"I saw Steven the other day. He was at a party that Chase took me to."

"Oh?" Her mother took the sandwich out of the pan and plated it for her. "Did you speak to him?"

"He spoke to me. He said that I was using Chase because I realized that I was never going to make it, that I couldn't be successful without a successful man to pull me up."

"You know that's all total crap, don't you?"

"I do. But I also know that other people think that of me. They see me, someone who is up to her ears in student loan debt, with her car that won't start and her job in a coffee shop, and they think that a woman like me doesn't belong with Chase Drayson. That I'm just using him."

"Since when do you care what other people think?"

"I don't. But that's not why I broke up with him."

"You actually broke up with him? Oh, Amber!" Her mother left the stove and sat down at the table, her head cupped in her hands. "I thought you were just scared. But you actually did it. Why on earth would you give up such a good thing?"

"That's what he said." She looked at her mother, who seemed as though she was truly distressed by the news.

"Why?"

"I want to be his equal. I don't want to just be his

girlfriend. I want to be his partner. He's amazing, but I felt like he was doing everything for me and that I was doing nothing for him. I've got all these goals, you know. I've got all these dreams and I promised myself that I was never going to give them up for any man. I don't want to end up…" She trailed off.

"Like me?"

"No, Mama. That is not what I meant."

"Is it so wrong to be like me? Is it so wrong to be a wife and mother? Is it so wrong to have thirty-five years of happiness with the man of your dreams? I may have been just a seamstress. I may not be as impressive to you as you would like, but I'm not ashamed of who I am or any of the decisions I have made, and I never thought my own daughter would feel that way about me."

"But I'm not ashamed! I didn't mean it the way it came out. I'm sorry, Mama."

"I'm sorry, too." She got up. "I have to go. I need to pick up some dinner for your father. He's working the night court tonight."

"Mama…"

"Goodbye, honey." She kissed Amber's cheek before she walked out. And Amber wasn't sure she could feel any worse than she did right that moment.

Chase kept staring at the numbers on his screen, but for once he couldn't make heads or tails of them. He couldn't concentrate. He thought it might be better for him to go home and forget about working today since he had so much trouble getting anything done, but he disregarded that idea. There were signs of Amber all around his place. A nightgown in a drawer. A pair of shoes in his closet. The bracelet with her name on it still on his dresser.

Usually his home was his sanctuary but today it wasn't. There wasn't anyplace he could go that would make his thoughts stop from turning to her.

His office door crept open and he saw Mariah's fiancé, Everett, peeking his head in. "You look like hell," he said.

"I'm fine." He shook his head. Apparently Jackson hadn't told anyone else about him and Amber. He was glad his brother had stayed quiet. Chase had barely come to terms with the fact that she didn't want to be with him anymore. He sure as hell wasn't ready to tell anyone else about it.

"Hello, Everett. Is there something I can do for you, or are you just here visiting your future wife?"

"Amber asked me to be here. She said she needed to talk to all of us."

"What?"

"Yeah." Mariah walked in, her eyes softening and lingering on Everett before she looked back at him. "She said it was important for all of us to be here. Do you know what she's talking about?"

"No," he said truthfully. She had broken up with him for some reason he still couldn't grasp, but he didn't think she would call a meeting to tell everyone that.

"Oh…" Mariah sighed. "I'm a little worried about her. I saw her when she came in. She just didn't look happy."

Jackson walked in with Amber then, and Chase's

stomach dropped. Mariah was right when she said that she didn't look happy. But it was more than that. Her normally wild ringlets were gone. Her hair was pulled back. Her face looked almost pale. She wore all black. Not a single piece of jewelry adorned her.

He wanted to go over to her. To comfort her, but he couldn't. Because he was the reason she was feeling the way that she did.

"Amber..."

"You can sit down, Chase. This won't take very long. I just wanted to tell you all that I'm leaving. Everett, I would like to transfer to another store if I could, but if not, it's okay."

"Of course you can transfer, but I'm confused. I thought you loved it here."

"I did. I do. But I need to move on now."

"No," Chase said. "I can go back to my old job. You don't have to leave. I will."

"What?" Mariah shook her head. "You can't leave now, Chase. We have the Bite of Seattle coming up."

"Chase is not going anyway," Amber said. "I'm the one who has to leave."

"But we don't want you to leave, either. Why does anyone have to leave?"

"Because I have to."

"It's because we broke up," Chase said, surprised at how angry he felt about it.

"Is that true?" Mariah looked between Chase and Amber. "But why? You were so happy."

"We were," Chase said. He wanted her to give them an explanation because he was still unclear as to why she couldn't be with him. He would never stop her from pursuing her dreams. He would be with her every step of the way.

"I want you to stay, Chase." She looked him in the eye as hers filled with tears. "I'm just the barista. Of course it makes sense for me to go."

"Damn it, Amber. You aren't just the barista. You are loved here."

"This is your family, though. I didn't want a big discussion. I just wanted to tell you all that I'm leaving. Everett, please call me when you have a spot. Mariah, we'll stay in touch. I have to go now."

She walked out of the room without another word.

"What happened, Chase?" Mariah turned to him. "I asked you not to get involved with my friend because I knew this was going to happen."

"I didn't do anything wrong."

"No? Then why is Amber walking around heartbroken? Why does she want to leave here?"

"She doesn't deserve to be treated poorly, Chase." Everett scowled at him, and that's when Chase lost his cool.

"She broke up with me, damn it! I'm in love with her and I'm tired of everyone treating me like I'm the bad guy here when the only thing I wanted to do was spend my life with her."

"Chase is right," Jackson spoke up for the first time. "You've been on his ass about Amber the whole time. He's our brother. Where is your loyalty?"

"I am loyal. That's why I didn't want you dating her,

because I knew when things ended, I would have to choose you over her. I didn't want to lose my friend."

"You don't have to lose her."

"What happened? Why did she break up with you? We were just with you two the other day."

"I've known Amber for a long time," Everett said. "I've never seen her as happy as she was with you."

"I'm not sure what happened. She ran into her ex at my work function and she broke up with me ten minutes later."

"What did she say exactly?" Mariah placed a comforting hand on his shoulder.

"Something about her goals and not being ready for a relationship."

"Do you think she still might be in love with her ex?" Jackson asked Everett, who had known Amber longer than all of them.

"I hope not. I've never met a more pretentious, self-righteous ass in my life. Amber is so full of life and that guy tried to squash that quality in her. Since she dumped him she has been more driven than ever."

"She's been working too hard. She's nearly been running herself ragged," Chase said.

"I agree." Everett nodded. "She needs to relax."

"He constantly put her down," Mariah said. "He didn't treat her jewelry design seriously. She told me he was controlling, that she didn't realize how much so until she completely lost herself. She promised herself that she would never lose herself to gain a man."

"I believe in her," Chase said. "I think she's amazing."

"But maybe she doesn't believe you believe in her. You've got to talk to her, Chase. You've got to do something to get her back."

"Why should I bother? I've done nothing but try with her. I'm not going to demean myself by going after someone who clearly wants nothing to do with me."

Amber knocked on her parents' door. She had just started working at another branch of Myers Coffee Roasters that day. It was fine. Everett only hired good people, but it wasn't the same as working at Lillian's. She didn't feel the warmth as she walked through the door. The day didn't fly by because she wasn't working with her friends. There was no Chase there to get a glimpse of as she did her job. And for the first time being a barista felt like work to her.

Her father, David, answered the door. He was still in his uniform, still looking handsome and fit even though his sixtieth birthday was coming in a few months. "Hello, Amber!"

"Hey, Daddy." She smiled at him because he looked happy to see her. "It's been a while."

"I've been working a lot of overtime. Trying to save up some money. Come inside."

"Oh, are you?" She entered the living room and turned to face him. "Is everything okay?"

"Yes. Of course. Don't tell your mother, but I'm planning to take her on a month-long trip."

"Really? Where?"

"She told me that she's always wanted to see Ibiza. I had to look up where it was. Found out that it's an island off the coast of Spain. So I figured we could see Europe. London, Paris, Madrid. Maybe sneak in Venice to see those canals."

"That sounds wonderful. She'll love it."

"You think so?" He looked bashful.

"I know so. She's always wanted to see the world."

"I know. That's why I've kept working. I could have retired a few years ago. I've done my thirty years on the job, but I wanted to keep working so I could have enough money to really spoil your mother during this time in our lives. A man wants to spoil a woman. I wish I could have given her everything she dreamed of when we first met. It killed me that I couldn't, but your mother never minded that the only vacations we could afford involved piling you kids in the car and taking you to a motel overnight. She never complained that she had to wear shoes until they wore out or that she had to wear the same coat for three years. She always seemed so happy, even with just the little bit we had when we were first starting out. It makes me love her more. It makes me want to move mountains for her."

"You sacrificed, too, didn't you?"

"I don't want to call it sacrifice. Makes it sound like my life was miserable. We just did what we had to do to get by. Of course we could have gotten by better with two children instead of four, but your mother wanted a big family. And I loved coming home to you kids. You all were the best thing we've ever done together."

"You're sweet, Daddy." She kissed his cheek and suddenly felt foolish. For so long love and marriage had meant sacrifice to Amber, but each of her parents had given up something in order to gain something better. Something more meaningful. Something that made them happy.

And it made her doubt if she was doing the right thing with Chase. She had missed him so much she had doubted herself anyway, but speaking to her father made her wonder—even if she did achieve all her goals, would she be happy alone? She would have a career but would she have a meaningful life?

"Your mother is in the kitchen just about to start dinner."

"I hope she didn't get too far. I brought you guys something to eat."

"I hope it's shrimp and grits."

"Yes, sir. Today is your lucky day."

"You don't have to bring anything when you come over. We're just happy to see you."

"I know, but I like to do something nice for you two sometimes."

He nodded. "Go on and see your mother. I'm going to get changed out of my work clothes."

She found her mother with her head in the freezer. "Don't take anything out," Amber called out to her mother. "I made dinner for you."

"Oh." She shut the freezer door. "Hello, baby girl. I wasn't expecting you."

"I wanted to see you. I wanted to apologize."

"You don't have to. I never wanted to end up like my mother. Of course you don't want to end up like me. Don't worry about it."

"I don't want you to think I'm ashamed of you

though. I'm not. That's not what I meant. You had a good life with Daddy. A good marriage. So many people wish they could have what you have. I wish I could have what you have."

"Don't you think you could have had that with Chase?"

"Our lives are so different. I'm not sure I would fit into his world."

"How is it when it's just the two of you and there's no one else around?"

"Perfect," she said without hesitation. "Everything feels perfect."

"Then what's the problem?

"I can't be sure of his feelings. I can't be sure that he won't look at me one day and decide that I'm not good enough to be with him long-term. That the novelty of having a broke artsy girlfriend won't wear off."

"I could choke that Steven. He did a number on you."

Amber's cellphone went off. She was tempted to ignore it, but she glanced at her caller ID to see that it was Jackson calling. He never called her. "Hello?"

"There's been an accident involving Chase."

"What?" It felt as if the world stopped spinning in that moment. As if the floor had dropped from beneath her feet.

"I need you to come down to the hospital immediately."

Chapter 15

"This is ridiculous," Chase said, struggling to sit up. "I'm fine. I just want to go home."

"You can't go home." Jackson pushed him back down on the bed. "The doctors want to keep you overnight. And knowing you, you won't rest even if you do go home. You'll create expense reports or something else stupid that doesn't need to be done."

"Expense reports aren't stupid! Ouch." His head throbbed. His whole body throbbed, but that's what happened when a sixteen-year-old on a bike hit you at full speed.

He had gone out for a run in the park just to clear his head. He was listening to music, trying not to think about Amber, and the last thing he remembered was seeing the kid's scared face and then waking up in the hospital with his brother standing over him. "Just relax, Chase. The more you fight it, the worse you'll feel."

"Chase…" He looked up to see Amber standing just inside of his room. Her eyes filled with tears immediately. He was surprised to see her there. He had told Jackson not to call anyone because he didn't want his family to worry, but Amber was there, looking terrified. "What happened?"

"It looks worse than it is."

She pushed past Jackson and gingerly placed her hand on his cheek. "It looks like you're a mummy." She kissed the small piece of his forehead that wasn't covered by a bandage.

"I just had a little run-in with a kid on a bike when I was in the park."

"A witness said he flew five feet in the air and skidded across the ground," Jackson said. "If he'd hit his head a little harder, he wouldn't be talking to us now."

Amber gasped as the tears started to roll down her face.

"Jackson!" He barked and then winced as his stiches pulled.

"Honey." Amber lightly kissed his lips a half dozen times. "I'm so sorry."

"He's got fifteen stitches in his head and a dislocated shoulder and he won't take his pain medication."

"Why not?" Amber looked into his eyes, hers still filled with tears.

"I don't need it."

"But you're in pain."

"I'm fine. I just want to go home."

"They want to keep him overnight," Jackson supplied.

"Will you shut up!" he barked at his brother, wanting to smack him.

"She needed to know." He shrugged.

"The only thing you succeeded in doing was making her cry."

"I'm fine. Stop arguing with your brother. Jackson, I know you're trying to help, but go do something with yourself. You're annoying the injured man."

"Okay." He squeezed her shoulder. "I'm going to go out and get some food. I'll bring you something back."

"Thanks for calling me, Jackson."

"I didn't do it for you. I did it for him. He needs you," he said as he walked out.

He wanted to protest Jackson's last comment. He wanted to think that he didn't need her, but even he had to admit that he felt better now that she was here, calmer. It had only been a couple of days since he had last seen her, but he missed her. He missed her to the point that it was painful. "Can I get you anything?" Amber asked as she pulled his blanket up over him. "You want me to go home and get your pajamas and a change of clothes for tomorrow?"

"You don't have to do that."

"Yes, I do. And anything else that you want or need. You just tell me and I'll make it happen."

"Will you stay here with me tonight?"

She looked him in the eye. "Of course I will. I wasn't planning on leaving."

"But you left me before."

She looked pained by his words, but she nodded. "Just because I broke up with you doesn't mean I'm not in love with you."

She told him she loved him so easily, as if it was the most natural thing in the world. And he believed her. He knew he was loved when he looked into her eyes, but it wasn't as easy for him to say. He had never been in love before. He had never said those words to a woman. His whole life he had been saving up those words. He wanted to say them when the time was right, when he really meant them. He didn't want to tell her when she had one foot out the door. He didn't want those words to go to waste.

"Come here." She leaned closer, allowing him to cup her face in his hands and kiss her. He ignored the twinges of pain in his head and the ache that shot up his arm when he moved it. Kissing her right then, feeling her soft sweet mouth open beneath his was more important. It made him forget where he was, forget the pain he was in, the pain he had been in the past few days without her.

"I'm assuming, since you can make out, that we shouldn't be too worried about your health."

Chase heard his mother's voice penetrate his fog, but he didn't pull away from Amber immediately, not wanting the moment to end.

But Amber turned away from him, her hands over her mouth, clearly embarrassed about being caught. "Mrs. Drayson. Hello again. I'm sorry. I'm just glad Chase is okay."

"I'm sure you are, dear. Amber, I would like for you to meet my husband, Graham."

"Hello, Mr. Drayson. I wish I could be meeting you under better circumstances."

"It's nice to meet you, Amber. Chase has only wonderful things to say about you."

"Oh." She glanced back at him. "That's nice to hear."

"How are you, son?" His father walked over and touched the shoulder he'd dislocated, causing Chase to flinch.

"I'm sorry." He stepped away from him.

"I've got some road rash. Don't worry about it. I told Jackson not to call you. But he seems hell bent on worrying everyone that I love."

"He told us you were okay, but you can't expect us not to come," his mother said as she kissed his cheek. "We're your parents. How are you feeling?"

"He's in a lot of pain," Amber answered for him. "But he's too macho to admit it. And he won't take the medicine that was offered to him."

"He's just like his father. The man broke his wrist once. Refused to go to the doctor. Refused to admit it was hurting. We only found out it was broken when it swelled to three times its normal size." Nadia paused and studied Amber for a moment. "That is a beautiful hair clip you're wearing. I don't think I've seen anything like it."

Amber touched her hair as if she were trying to remember what she had in it. "Oh, this?" She slipped it out and handed it to Nadia who studied it closer. "I made that. You can keep it. I have a bunch of them."

"You made this?" She blinked at Amber.

"Yes. The blue stone is lapis lazuli. But if you prefer a more precious stone, I could do that, too."

"This work is exquisite. It's so detailed. I can't believe you made this by hand. The work must be painstaking."

"I love it, Mrs. Drayson. Designing jewelry is what I wanted to do since I was a little girl."

Chase could hear the love for it in her voice. He knew that she did. He knew that growing her business was why she broke up with him. She loved him, but she needed to make a name for herself even more.

"You didn't have to come home with me," Chase said to Amber the next day as she was unlocking his front door.

"Yes, I did." She didn't feel right leaving him just yet. She wasn't sure she was going to feel right leaving him ever, but right now she knew her conscience wouldn't let her walk away from him. Not now that he was hurt. She had stayed by his side in the hospital all night, watching him sleep in fits because he was in pain.

She could have lost him. The kid could have been going a little faster. Chase could have landed a little harder, could have landed a little differently and broken his neck. She tried not to think of all of the could-haves. He was here now and she was grateful for it.

As soon as they both stepped inside, she kissed him as deeply as she could manage without hurting him.

"I don't want you to leave," he told her when she broke the kiss, and she wasn't sure if he was asking her to stay the night or stay forever. So she just nodded. "The doctor said you could take a hot bath tonight. It'll ease your aches and pains."

He grasped her chin between his fingers and kissed her, sucking her lower lip into her mouth, which turned her on immediately. "You can ease my aches and pains."

"You can't possibly be thinking about sex right now. You were in a horrible accident. You dislocated your shoulder."

"You make me forget the pain," he said, kissing the side of her neck.

Her eyes closed unwillingly as she fell under his spell. "I look awful and I need to shower."

"You smell good to me." He wrapped his good arm around her waist. "But if you're worried about it. I'm sure you'll get plenty clean in the bathtub with me."

"You need to rest. You need to heal. You need to stop kissing me!"

"I can't help myself. I've missed you."

"I missed you, too." She never wanted to have to miss him again, but she wondered if after he healed, after they had been together for a while, would he still feel the way he did right now? She must have told him that she loved him a dozen times since she first saw him yesterday, but she couldn't help but note that he hadn't once said that he loved her back.

There was a knock at Chase's door two days later and he eased himself off the couch to answer it. It was one of the few times he'd had to get up to do anything for himself since he'd returned home from the hospital. Amber had been by his side for the past three days. He'd thought he would have returned to work by now, but as all the adrenaline had worn off, the soreness had kicked in and he could barely move without discomfort or outright pain. But Amber had been there, making life easier for him, taking care of him when normally he would have suffered through this himself.

She was taking care of him. He wasn't used to anyone taking care of him. He was the one who made sure everyone was all right, that he was there when anyone else needed something. It was out of his comfort zone to be on the receiving end, and there had been more than a few times when he'd tried to do things for himself, just to spare her the trouble, but she hadn't let him.

For once let me do something for you.

Those words struck him. Throughout their relationship he had wanted to do things for her. He wanted to be the one who took care of her, who bought her things, who supported her, and she had been uncomfortable about it.

Now he could see why. Now he understood a little more about her. They were more similar than they were different. And it made him love her even more.

He finally made his way to the door, expecting to see one of his family members, but instead he saw a woman he recognized but had never met. "Mrs. Bernard."

"Oh! You know who I am?"

"Yes, come in." She looked like Amber. That kind of sweet, earthy beauty that was achieved only by good genetics. "I recognize you from your picture."

"How are you feeling? Amber was incredibly concerned about you."

"I'm sore, but I'll be fine. She isn't here. She went out to buy me a new heating pad."

She nodded. "She's a good girl. I just stopped by to bring you some of my world famous banana pudding and to wish you a speedy recovery."

"Thank you. I appreciate that."

Mrs. Bernard opened her mouth as if she wanted to say something, but then she shut it.

"What is it?" Chase prompted.

"I know it's not my place to ask, but are you and Amber back together again?"

"That's a good question. I don't know. I'm not sure that anything has changed for her."

"Can we sit down for a minute? I need to tell you something about Amber."

"Of course." He motioned to his couch the best he could with his stiff, sore body. "Please, tell me."

"Did she ever tell you what happened between her and Steven?"

"No. I just know that it didn't end well."

"He's older than she is, by quite a lot. And when she first met him, he was successful. He dazzled her. She looked up to him for advice and guidance and pretty soon her entire world revolved around him. Out of all my children, Amber was my dreamer. She had all these huge plans for herself. These big goals and dreams, but when she was with him, they all sort of faded away and the only dreams she had left were Steven's. Little by little he started to control her. Who she could be friends with. Where she worked. It got to the point where she would only wear things that he liked to see her in. He made her feel like nothing she had ever done was good enough. My strong-willed little girl was living her life for this idiot of a man. He would talk down to her, manipulate her. I was worried about her. But then something switched on for her, and she was able to see Steven as the petty, self-centered ass he was. She grew up and when she left him she swore that she would never let another man have that much control over her life. She never wanted to fall in love again. Because to her, love made her weak. Love and marriage meant sacrifice to her."

"Oh." He wasn't sure what to say to that. It all made so much sense now. She was afraid he was going to disappoint her. "I'm not him."

"I know you aren't."

"I'm in love with your daughter."

"I know that. But I'm not sure she does."

"How can I prove it?"

"Hmm. Point in the direction of your kitchen."

"It's over there. Why do you need to know?"

"So I can grab some spoons. Banana pudding is brain food, my boy, and we need to think."

Chapter 16

"Are you sure you're going to be okay alone until I get home later tonight?" Amber looked at Chase, who was standing behind her as she opened his front door. She had to leave him tonight to go teach her class at the community center. She hadn't been to work all week so she could take care of Chase, but she didn't want to miss class with her girls unless it was absolutely necessary. She had missed her meeting with the owner of that jewelry store, but she didn't feel bad about it because Chase was more important. She had formed a picture in her mind of what her life might be like in thirty years. In that picture she saw a husband, a happy family, a home filled with love. Her jewelry would always be important to her, but opportunities would come and go. Another Chase wouldn't walk into her life. The thought of walking out that door and leaving him had her stomach in knots. Chase seemed to be feeling better physically. He promised her he was fine, but he had been extremely quiet all day. Not distant, just quiet. Almost thoughtful...and she'd wanted to ask him a dozen times what was running through his head.

"Don't worry."

"You had Jackson take you to the doctor instead of me this morning. It makes me wonder if there is something wrong that you are not telling me."

"I'm fine." He pulled her into him and gave her a long, deep kiss. "I'm going to show you how fine I am as soon as you get home."

Home. They both kept using the word this week. And when she was with him it felt like home, but she didn't live here. She had a life on hold. Her jewelry that was sitting unfinished with clients waiting for it. She had to get back to that life, but she didn't want to leave him. "I love you," she said one more time.

"I'm lucky to be loved by you."

She smiled at him, but she was feeling a little sad because she wanted him to say it back. She needed to hear him say it back that time. It was what she needed in order to know if this relationship could move forward or not.

She got to the center early for a staff meeting that ended up being canceled. She was glad for the extra time she had before her class started. It was time away from Chase to think, away from his soothing deep voice and his warm arms. They hadn't discussed their relationship once, what he wanted from her, what was next.

Part of her was tempted to let it go. To just be with him as long as she possibly could before it ended. Because she didn't think she could walk away from him right now. She didn't want to see him hurt again.

"Excuse me, Amber?" She looked up to see Nadia Drayson just inside her classroom and for a moment she was too stunned to speak.

"Mrs. Drayson. Hello. I—I… Are you meant to be here?"

"Yes, Amber. I don't often go to places I'm not meant to be. I came to see you."

"I hope this isn't one of those 'stay away from my son or else' conversations—frankly, after the past few days, I'm not up to it."

Nadia laughed and Amber was once again blown away by how beautiful she was. She was elegant in a way that Amber could never dream of being and in her she saw little bits of Chase, Jackson and Mariah. "Of course I'm not here to tell you to stay away from Chase. Although, I was surprised when I learned that you had broken up with him. You two didn't seem very broken up at the hospital. A blind person could see how much you love him."

"Is it that obvious? Do I look like one of those pathetic, love-struck women with her heart in her eyes?"

"Yes, but only a little. A mother likes to see that for her son. It's nice to know that he has a woman who will stick by him in bad times." Nadia walked closer. "What if I told you that Chase got wiped out by a bad investment and he's starting from scratch again?"

"Really?" Amber perked up. "That would make it easier for me to love him."

Nadia laughed again. "I must say I was expecting some kind of worry to cross your face, or maybe sheer terror, but you said the last thing I would expect any woman to say."

"I don't want anyone to think that I'm with him for what he has. And I don't want him to support me. I want to be his equal. His partner. I want to take care of him as much as he wants to take care of me."

"And you do that. You take care of his soul and his spirit. My son is truly happy with you and that is priceless."

"You don't think he's too good for me?"

"He's my firstborn. I think he's too good for everyone. But if I had to choose for him, I would choose you. And that's why I'm doing this for you." She reached into her bag and handed her a piece of paper with a name and address on it. "Chase called me yesterday, asking me if I knew anyone with connections in the jewelry world because he knew you missed your meeting with the store owner while you were nursing him. I told him I didn't, but I do and I had already showed the piece you gave me to my friend who is a buyer for all the Fine's department stores in this region. She loved this piece and wants to start out with an order of one hundred. She wants to see what else you can do, so bring your best work."

Amber just looked at Nadia, feeling near tears and not sure what to say. "*Thank-you* doesn't seem like a big enough word."

"You don't have to thank me." She touched Amber's arm. "Just make my son happy."

"Why didn't you want him to know about your contact?"

"I didn't want you or him to think that he was doing this for you. I believe in your work and I feel strongly that women need to help each other out when they can. But Chase believes in you. I hope you realize that. My son has never come to me for help before and that's a testament to how much he loves you."

"Can I hug you?"

"I think that would be appropriate."

"Thank you." She hugged her tightly, feeling a rush of love for the woman she barely knew.

"You're welcome. I expect a one-of-a-kind piece for the charity ball I'm throwing next month. I would like the stones to be emerald to match my dress. And make sure you have a gown. I think tangerine would look lovely on you."

"Maybe you can go shopping with me?"

"We'll bring Mariah and make it a day." She pulled away from her and left, leaving Amber still feeling a little dazed about what had just happened.

Her students started to funnel in a few minutes later and she started her class. She was in the middle of discussing the upcoming craft fair when there was a knock at the door. She looked up to see Jackson walk in with a large tray, followed by Mariah with bottles of non-alcoholic sparkling cider. Her mother walked in, too, and then Chase who was carrying a small bakery box.

"What are you all doing here?"

"We wanted the kids to try out our new cupcake flavors." Chase kissed her cheek.

"You came up with a flavor?"

"Yes."

"And you didn't tell me? We've been working on this for weeks!"

He grinned at her and kissed her cheek again, which prompted some giggles from her students.

"I told you he was her boyfriend," one of them said.

"Help us pass these out," Chase said to her.

"Okay." She studied the cupcakes, which had a beautiful thick white icing and a very yellow cake and what looked to be a dash of cinnamon on top. "Mariah, did you bake these? They are beautiful."

"It's Chase's recipe. He did a beautiful job decorating them, too. If I had known he was good at this, I would have had him in the kitchen a long time ago.

"When did you have time to do this? How did you do this?"

"This is what I was doing when I told you I was at the doctor. Your mother helped."

"Mom?" Amber looked at her mother who was busy pouring cider.

"They used my kitchen." She shrugged.

"I learned a few things from her," Mariah said. "I'll be calling your mother for more advice."

"What? You were there, too?"

"Of course. I had to be there. This was important."

"Why wasn't I invited?" she asked, feeling a little bewildered.

"Because I wanted to surprise you." He handed her

the bakery box that he had carried in. "These are just for you."

"We'll take these home. I'll just grab one of the left-over ones from the tray." She turned away from him, took one of the cupcakes off the tray and sank her teeth into it. "Wow." She looked at Chase. "This is my ma-ma's banana pudding! You made this?" she said, tak-ing another bite. "This is amazing. How did you come up with the idea?"

"You were right. I stopped thinking so hard about it and it came to me. I was eating your mother's home-made banana pudding and thought this would be per-fect."

"It was smart."

"Thank you. Now can you stop ruining my pro-posal?"

"What?" She wasn't sure she had heard him right, but her heart was pounding uncontrollably.

Chase went down on his knee, a gorgeous grin on his face. "Open the cupcake box." He handed it back to her.

"Oh." Her eyes filled with tears. There were two rows of mini cupcakes spelling out the words *Marry Me*. She looked back down at him and he was holding a diamond ring in his hand. She couldn't believe it. It was so soon. Just minutes before, she was wondering if their relationship could ever last and now he was be-fore her, asking her to be his wife. "You want to marry me?" she whispered.

"I had no concept of what love really was until I met you. I think I fell in love with you the first time you smiled at me. You make me think about life in a different way. You make me happier than I have ever been and there is no one else in the world I would rather be with. So please, Amber, will you marry me?"

There were a hundred practical reasons to say no, but she couldn't think of any of them right now. She only knew that she wanted to be with him, that life without him was unbearable. "I love you, Chase. I want to spend the rest of my life loving you. Of course I'll marry you." Chase got to his feet and pulled her into a long kiss. There was an explosion of cheers from their family and the girls.

"I want the world for you," he whispered in her ear. "Your dreams are my dreams and I'm going to do everything I can to make sure they come true."

"I want to do something for you, Chase. But there is nothing I can think of that's enough."

"You can love me. That's enough. You can let me love you and spoil you sometimes and give you things because that will make me happy."

"I know. I'm a work in progress. Promise you'll be patient with me."

"I'll promise if you let me take you away."

"Take me away?"

"First on a pre-honeymoon to Snoqualmie Falls. Next to see the world. I want to see the world with you. My whole life I was looking for someone to have an adventure with and now I've found that person in you."

"I love you." She kissed him. "I'm excited. We are going to have one hell of a great journey."

* * * * *

JUST CAN'T GET ENOUGH?

Join our social communities
and talk to us online.

You will have access to the latest
news on upcoming titles and special
promotions, but most importantly,
you can talk to other fans about your
favorite Harlequin reads.

Harlequin.com/Community

 Facebook.com/HarlequinBooks

Twitter.com/HarlequinBooks

Pinterest.com/HarlequinBooks

*Four years ago Kara Goshay believed a vicious lie
about Virgil Bougard and ended their relationship.
And even after her apology, Virgil is still bitter.
Now his family firm has hired Kara's PR company to
revamp his playboy image. But faking a liaison with
Kara for the media backfires when the line between
fantasy and reality is blurred by strong sexual
attraction. The stakes are high—but so is their searing
desire, a connection so intense it could possibly tame
this elusive, unforgiving bachelor at last...*

*Read on for a sneak peek at
BACHELOR UNFORGIVING, the next exciting
installment in* New York Times *bestselling author
Brenda Jackson's* BACHELORS IN DEMAND *series!*

His eyes were so cold she felt the icy chill all the way to
her bones. She took a deep breath and then said, "Hello,
Virgil."

He didn't return her greeting, just continued to give
her a cold stare. But she pushed on. "May I speak with
you privately for a minute?"

"No. We have nothing to say to each other."

Virgil's tone was so hard Kara was tempted to turn
and walk away. But she refused to do that. She would

get him alone even if she had to provoke him into it. She lifted her chin, met his gaze and smiled ruefully. "I understand you not wanting to risk being alone with me, Virgil. Especially since you've never been able to control yourself where I'm concerned."

The narrowing of Virgil's eyes indicated she might have gone too far by bringing up their past relationship and reminding him of how taken he'd once been with her.

He continued to stare at her for the longest time. Silence surrounded the group, and she figured Virgil was well aware the two of them had not only drawn the attention of his godbrothers but a few others in the room who'd known they'd once been a hot item.

Finally Virgil slowly nodded. "You want to talk privately, Kara?" he asked in a clipped voice that was shrouded with a daring tone, one that warned she might regret the request. "Then, by all means, lead the way."

Don't miss BACHELOR UNFORGIVING
by Brenda Jackson, available August 2016
wherever Harlequin® Kimani Romance™
books and ebooks are sold!